rial i·
ary

A Study on Papuan Music

AMS PRESS
NEW YORK

I. The Kauwerawèt (Van Rees-mountains) singing in the grammophone.

EXPEDITION TO THE CENTRAL MOUNTAINS (NASSAU-RANGE) IN THE NETHERLANDS EAST INDIES 1926.

A Study on Papuan Music

written at the hand of phonograms recorded
by the ethnographer of the expedition, Mr.
C. C. F. M. Le Roux, and of other data,

by

J. KUNST

with 63 pen and ink drawings by Mas
Pirngadi, made principally from exhibits
at the Museum of the Royal Batavia Society
of Arts and Sciences, and from drawings,
published elsewhere; a map of the distribution of the instrumental forms found in New
Guinea and the adjacent territories, and 2
reproductions of photographs.

V.

*The Netherlands East Indies Committee for
Scientific Research*

Printed by
G. Kolff & Co. at Weltevreden, D.E.I.
1931.

Library of Congress Cataloging in Publication Data

Kunst, Jaap, 1891–1960.
    A study on Papuan music.

    Reprint of the 1931 ed. printed by G. Kolff,
Weltevreden, D.E.I., which was issued as no.
5 of Netherlands East Indies Committee for
Scientific Research. [Publication]
    At head of original title: Expedition to the
central mountains (Nassau-Range) in the Netherlands
East Indies, 1926.
    Bibliography: p.
    1. Music, Papuan—History and criticism.
2. Music, Primitive.   3. Musical instruments—
New Guinea.   I. Title.   II. Series: Indisch
comité voor wetenschappeliike onderzoekingen.
[Publicaties]; 5.
ML3547.K9   1978   781.7′95   75-35130
ISBN 0-404-14146-3

First AMS edition published in 1978.

Reprinted from the edition of 1931, Weltevreden, D.E.I.
Trim size and text area have been slightly altered in
this edition. Original trim size: 18 × 26.5 cm. Text area:
11 × 18.5 cm.

I N D E X

§ 1.

INTRODUCTION.

It is a somewhat onerous task to write about exotic music, when one has not heard and felt it in its appropriate surroundings. The tissue of factors, which create the peculiar atmosphere: the devotion and concentration of the musicians, the contact between the performers and the audience, the native conditions, the influence of the hour and the season — these cannot be recreated, when listening to records taken by another person. For the phonograph, however excellent, and even indispensible a medium, only reproduces the sounds correctly, — and undoubtedly, this is the most important factor, when one is conducting musical investigations, — but it cannot reproduce the invaluable, intangible, psychic atmosphere, which surrounds this music, when heard on its "native heath".

Nevertheless I felt bound to comply with Mr. Le Roux's request, to make a study, as complete as lay in my power, of the melodies and phonograms he had brought back from New Guinea, because I am convinced of the great interest of such investigations, and also, because I knew, that anybody else, when undertaking this task, would be faced with the same difficulties.

1

The making and analysing of this kind of records cannot be done quickly and minutely enough. VON HORNBOSTEL very rightly says: "The few thousand phonographic records hitherto collected in museums and archives are only a beginning; they are haphazard fragments, instead of giving a general view. *What we need above all is to register systematically the musical material of all peoples of the world by means of the phonograph*"[1]). And what this musicologist says in the same paper about African music, might be said with equal justice of the music of a large part of the East Indian Archipelago, and of the South Sea Islands: "It is ...... to be feared, that the modern efforts to protect culture are coming too late. As yet we hardly know what African music is. If we do not hasten to collect it systematically and to record it by means of the phonograph, we shall not even learn what it was"[2]).

When studying the literature about New Guinea, one cannot help being struck by the fact, that there are almost as many opinions about the descent and the ethnic composition of the Papuans, as there are ethnologists, who have faced these problems[3]). On

---

1)   VON HORNBOSTEL. VI p. 4 a. f.
2)   ibid.   p. 33.
3)   See f. i. SELIGMANN I p. 246 a. f.; GRAEBNER I; the Encyclopaedia Brittannica, 11th. ed. (1911) vol. 20 p. 741 s. v. Papuans; RECHE p. 481; Exploratieverslag ps. 220—235; the Encyclopaedia of the Neth. Indies, vol. III, 2nd. ed., p. 298 s. v. Papoea's; KLEIWEG DE ZWAAN ps. 23—27 and WIRZ II ps. 5—8.

one point, however, there seems to be perfect agreement, viz. that the population of this huge island is not unmixed, or even homogeneous in its component parts, but that these hundreds of larger and smaller tribes possess, in different mixtures, the elements of various races, and that different strata of culture are to be found here, superimposed the one upon the other.

The music of these regions seems to confirm that heterogeneous character fully. The study of this object, nevertheless, has not yet shed much light on this chaos. The investigations are still too few, the insufficiently, or even still entirely unexplored territories still too large, to expect musicology to be, as yet, of great assistance in solving the riddle of the Papuans, — if it will ever be possible to find a way out of this ethnological labyrinth [4]).

Still, I venture to suggest, that, from what little musical material the various expeditions have brought back from this part of the world (and that generally as a mere ''by-product'') [5]), valuable indications may be obtained. The expedition of 1926, thanks to

---

[4] Much interest may be felt in the results of the analysis of Papuan phonograms, now being conducted at the Berlin Phonogram Archives by Dr. KOLINSKI.

[5] It was impossible for me to consult the whole of the New Guinea literature, as only the library of the Royal Batavia Society, which however contains a splendid collection of books on this subject, was available for me.

Mr. LE ROUX, certainly has amply done its part in furthering our object, as will be shown hereafter [6]).

Even after a superficial study of the musical material, collected by Mr. LE ROUX during the expedition, one arrives at the conclusion, that it may rationally be divided into two parts : on the one hand the music of the Kauwerawèt from the Van Rees Mountains, and on the other the music of the pygmoid tribes from the Central Mountains. This division is based, not so much on the locality, as on the great difference in character of these musical effusions. There is no more convincing proof of the fact, that up to the present day there are in New Guinea several kinds of music existing side by side, which cannot be explained or looked upon as successive phases of development, than a comparison between these two groups of melodies just mentioned, or, to put it in a more general way : the comparison between these two melodic groups proves, that more than one civilization has made its influence felt in the cultural development of the Papuans.

Involuntarily one imagines a more or less original

6) This paper was nearly finished before the publication of SACHS's "Geist und Werden der Musikinstrumente". After reading this masterly monograph I have brought some modifications in my instrumental divisions, so that they may better compared with those of SACHS. I therefore subdivided originally undivided instrumental groups into more narrowly circumscribed groups, f.i. the panpipes into "raft"-pipes and "bundle"-pipes; the trumpets and shellconchs into instruments with a lateral blowing-hole, and those with a blowing-hole at the apex. Finally, in the index for the distribution map, each instrumental form has been given, as far as possible, the number of the cultural stratum to which it has been assigned by SACHS.

population, which has retreated into its mountain fastnesses, driven back by another more civilized and stronger race from overseas. However, before following up this train of thought, it is better to examine the melodies brought by the 1926 expedition, and to compare them, as far as possible, with the material already published.

———

THE MUSIC OF THE KAUWERAWET.

A. Vocal Music.

The Kauwerawèt (Takoetamesso)-melodies recorded, at least the vocal ones, were executed by four different persons, called respectively: Jacob (phon. I),
Komaha or Komasa (phon. II, III, IV, and XVI),
Bidjowa or Pidjowa (phon. V, VI and VII) and
Basakara (phon. XVI); phon. VIII was sung in unison
by the four together.

The records at our disposal — photograph nr. I gives
a picture of the actual taking of the records — only
contain three different tunes. As a result of this fort-
unate circumstance, we have more than one record of
each of them. We have a record of melody α (phon. I,
II, III and VI), sung respectively by Jacob, Komasa — who sang·it twice, on different occasions — and
Pidjowa; melody β (phon. V, VII and VIII) sung
respectively by Pidjowa — twice, on different occasions — and by the four together; melody γ (phon.
IV and XVI) respectively by Komasa, and by him
and Basakara together.

These three tunes are all very short, so that they
could be taken several times on one wax cylinder,
every time with a different text. This text may be

called strophical, but the metre is rather free; the number of syllables in one line varies considerably[7]), and naturally this affects the rhythm of the melody.

These factors made it possible to determine, which parts of these melodies should be considered as essential, and which parts as variable.

In most cases it was possible to fix the height of the tones sung quite definitely. Of course this applies in the first place to those tones that may be considered as principal tones: in melody β these are the key-note (if we may call it that), its lower fourth and its lower octave; in melody γ four of the five tones used. Of the remaining tones of these two melodies the intonation was not quite constant, and could only be determined approximately. They have been put between brackets in the table of measurements below. In one case only (phon. IV) it proved to be impossible for *one* of the tones (which occurs only very occasionally and unstressed) to determine the number of vibrations.

In melody α all the tones were easily measurable.

The performance of this melody α, and occasionally also of melody β, is interwoven with birds' voices. Especially Komasa is an expert in this respect; more or less sweet twitterings alternate with highly realistic turkey-like gobblings and the quacking of ducks.

VAN DER SANDE[8]) writes about the playing of the sacred flutes of Nacheibe (N. E. Neth. New Guinea),

7) Compare LE ROUX ps. 507/8.
8) N. G. III p. 296.

that the players often imitate the voices of certain birds [9]). From this he concludes, that perhaps these birds play a certain part in the religious ideas. It is therefore possible, that the occurrence of similar sounds also in the *singing* of these tribes finds its origin in their religion. PULLE [10]) records of the Pesechem, who inhabit the southern slopes of the Central Mountains in the neighbourhood of the Wilhelmina top, that they also weave into their songs the voices of animals by way of musical ornament. According to the verbal statements of Mr. LE ROUX, the tribes, he visited in the Nassau Range, symbolize consciously certain animals by means of their Jew's harp, and this is not always done, as one would be inclined to suppose, by imitating the call or the cry of the animal in question, but also by producing other sounds, which, to the uninitiated ear, seem to have no connection with the animal at all.

To the ear and eye, trained to European melody, the most remarkable characteristic of these tunes is, beside theirs shortness, their tendency to descend the scale. This is a common trait in primitive melody [11]). Henceforth it will be styled in this article as "tiled" music.

---

9) See further p. 23.
10) PULLE p. 191. Compare also WIRZ II ps. 118/9.
11) "In purily melodic songs certain natural traits have maintained themselves which in our harmonic music have been superimposed upon or supplanted by other traits. They are "natural", i.e. rooted in the psychophysical constitution of man, and can therefore be found all over the world. The natural motion of melody is downward; like breathing or striking, from tension to rest." (VON HORNBOSTEL V p. 7).

The type of this Kauwerawèt music is ''Australian''. Similar melodies are met with, besides in Australia, on the islands of Torres Straits[12]), and in British New Guinea among the tribes of Beagle Bay[13]). After the style with narrow intervals of the Wedda and of some of the tribes of Terra del Fuego, it is undoubtedly the most primitive known up to the present day[14]).

The rhythmic forms are simple. As a rule one hears every time some tones of small values, followed by a longdrawn note, generally a lower one. It depends upon the text, whether there appear 16th figures or quintoles or trioles. The frequent use of the latter, as shown in melodies β and γ, has already been observed in other parts of the Papuan territories, viz. by WILLIAMS for the Orakaiva (Brit. New Guinea)[15]), by MYERS for the islands in Torres Straits[16]), by VAN DER SANDE for the inhabitants of Humboldt Bay[17]), and by JONGEJANS for those of the Central Mountains[18]). I myself heard 6/8 figures and trioles in the songs of the inhabitants of Humboldt Bay and Japèn at the Ethnographical Exhibition at Weltevreden in May 1929.

---

12) Myers passim.
13) Statement by Prof. VON HORNBOSTEL.
14) For a sketch of the development of melody, see VON HORNBOSTEL III and LACHMANN; here we find collected typical examples of successive stages of development.
15) WILLIAMS III p. 38.
16) C. A. E. ps 244/7 and 262/3.
17) N. G. III p. 309 (as a figure of the drum-accompaniment to the dance).
18) See hereafter p. 25.

However, this use of the ternary rhythm is not a peculiarity which distinguishes the Papuan music from that of the adjacent races, for it seems, that trioles are also very common in the music of the Queensland natives [19]), and they are not at all rare in Melanesian [20]) and Indonesian [21]) melody.

Before reproducing and analysing the melodies recorded, I want to say a few words about the material qualities of the records themselves. They are fairly plain, as regards the sound; as for rhythm, they present some difficulties, because occasionally they "derail" (a result of being played too often before being copied) and a few of them (probably because the gramophone was not quite steady during the making of the record) show an inclination to have a rhythm of their own. These obstacles could only be obviated by hearing the records very often and by comparing all the records at our disposal.

Melody α (Table I).
The form recorded here seems the most usual. Sometimes small non-essential rhythmical changes occur, especially in the second part of the melody;

---

19) "Globus" LVI p. 123; VON HORNBORSTEL III p. 21.

20) EBERLEIN ps. 641/2; VON HORNBOSTEL II blz. 492 and examples of melody Nos. 4, 6, 30 and 31.

21) In Javanese orchestral music they are heard especially in the gambang-kayu paraphrases. — For trioles of different values in Sundanese music see KUNST I Bijl. I and II. There in West-Java they are also found in many gamelan-Degung melodies. — On the island Nias the 6/8 time predominates generally in the songs and in the doli-doli- and druri-dana-melodies. — The same must be said with regard to the tunes of some Florinese tribes.

they are the result of irregularities in the text. Schematically the melodic structure may be represented by:

The measuring of the scale tones resulted in:

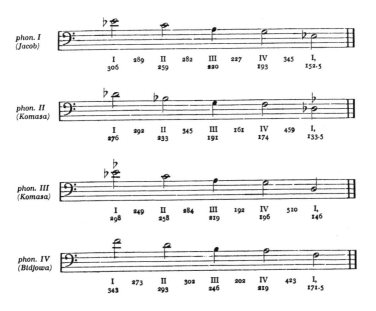

Jacob and Komasa take the lower octave-tone slightly flat. Bidjowa — of the four singers evidently the one endowed with the best ear (and, in my opinion, also with the best voice) — takes that tone perfectly true.

11

When we look for the average of the intervals, as sung, we find for the four phonograms:

I 275¾ II 303¼ III 195½ IV 449½ I_1 ,

and if we make the true octave, as undoubtedly it was meant to do, close the series, we get for the interval IV — I_1 : 425½ C.

If we omit phon. III, where Komasa seems rather below his usual form, the averages are:

I 284⅔ II 309⅔ III 196⅔ IV 429⅓ I_1 ,

and with the correction of the octave: IV 409 I_1 .

Without doing violence to this scale, we may therefore represent it as:

The compass of the melody is *one octave*.

Melody β , Entje Mararieo [22]) (Table I).

This melody is rendered with a number of non-essential variations, caused by the text. Schematically it may be represented by:

---

22) Le Roux ps. 507/8. The text tells of a bird-hunter, Entje, who came across the sea and was murdered in the interior on account of some love-affair.

As already mentioned, there are 3 phonograms of this melody. Measurements show, that the following scales have been used:

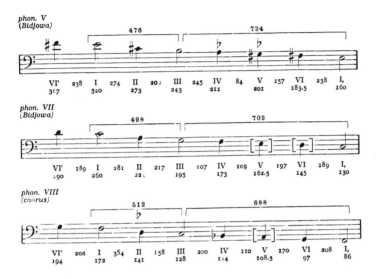

In these phonograms we find an almost pure fourth and fifth, and in phon. VII we find them even quite true (resp. 498 and 702 C.). This is also the case with the octave in all three phonograms.

The average of the intervals sung are:
I 303 II 192⅓ III 217⅓ IV 101 V 174⅔ VI 211⅔ I₁ .

So we may represent the scale in European notation as follows:

The compass of this melody does not exceed *one none*.

We may mention about phon. VIII, that the melody is started every time by one singer; at K the others join in. The four performers do not sing quite true, when singing in unison, and also their rhythm is rather jagged: according to our western ideas the performance is rather ''untidy'' [23]), as well from a melodic, as from a rhythmic point of view. Only the long-drawn notes are sung with a touching uniformity.

This peculiarity is a well-known characteristic of primitive music. The framework of the fourths and fifths is at a certain stage filled in with one or two tones, the intonation of which is of minor importance [24]).

---

23) ''Jeder singt, wie ihm der Schnabel gewachsen ist, ohne Rücksicht auf die Genauigkeit''. (SCHMIDT-ERNSTHAUSEN p. 269).

24) Compare VON HORNBOSTEL VI ps. 7/9. — Prof. VON HORNBOSTEL kindly sent me some written observations — bearing on the present article, of which I sent him a copy — among which the following on the manner in which the distance between two ''Gerüsttöne'' (framework-tones) — in this case a fourth or a fifth — is bridged over:

''Die einfachen Intervallverhältnisse, in denen ein grösseres Intervall durch einen unbetonten Zwischenton beim natürlichen Singen geteilt wird, sind Glieder der Reihe 12 : 12 : 7 : 5 : 2, d.h., die Centszahlen der Teilintervalle verhalten sich, ganz gleichgültig wie die absolute Grösse der Intervalle ist, so, wie im Maassstab der konsonanten Intervalle Oktave—Oktave—Quint—Quart—Ganzton. Durch die Konsonanz eben wird unter den (kontinuierlich variablen, daher unendlich vielen) Distanzsystemen (absoluten Grössen) eines ausgezeichnet. Die Intervalle dieses ausgezeichneten Systems sind gegeben durch die Verhältnisreihe der Schwingungszahlen 1 : 2 : 4 : 6 : 8 : 9, die Intervall-(Distanz-) Verhältnisse jedes beliebigen Systems aber durch die Reihe 1200 : 1200 : 702 : 498 : 204, oder angenähert, aber praktisch genau genug, durch 12 : 12 : 7 : 5 : 2.

Das Gesetz bestätigt sich auch an Ihren Messungen, in manchen Fällen sehr genau, so bei den Quartenteilungen nach 5 : 7.

Melody γ (Table I).

Of this melody also some variations have been recorded. A scheme of its structure is as follows:

Measuring the phonograms gave the following results:

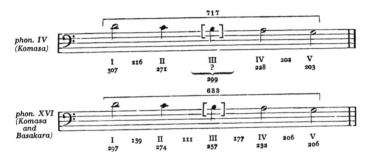

The average of the intervals sung comes to:

Note 24 (continued).

Phon. IV	gemessen	216	+ 299	= 515
	berechnet	215	+ 301	= 516
Phon. XVI	gem.	288	+ 206	= 494
	ber.	288	+ 206	= 494
Phon. VII	gem.	281	+ 217	= 498
	ber.	290½	+ 207½	= 498

Die ersten beiden Beispiele zeigen, wie bei verschiedener, von der reinen abweichender Grösse der Quart, die Teilungsproportion doch erhalten bleibt. Freilich ist in diesen Fällen auch das eine Teilintervall konsonant (204), sie sind also nicht beweisend für das Distanzgesetz. Dieses erklärt aber die Teilung nach 1 : 1 in

Phon. V	gemessen	241	+ 238	= 479
	berechnet	239½	+ 239½	= 479

und die Teilung nach 5 : 2 in

Phon. VIII	gem.	354	+ 158	= 512
	ber.	365	+ 146	= 511''

15

I 177½ II 293½ IV 204 V,

so that — and this especially as regards phon. IV — the scale (after transposition to C) may be rendered by:

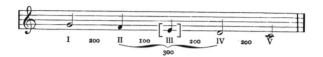

The compass of the melody, on phon. IV almost a pure fifth (717, instead of 702 C.), is much smaller on phon. XVI. Still, even then, the melody gives the impression of extending over a full fifth.

B. Flute Music.

From the whole of New Guinea we know a great many kinds of flutes [25]), but from the North coast of Neth. New Guinea we have only two types of which it is stated, that they are generally used. (A small signal flute, found in Witriwai and Humbolt Bay [26]),

---

25) See map.

26) SCHMELTZ V p. 243; Mus. Bat. Soc. No. 18059a; VAN DER SANDE pl. XXIX figs. 4 and 5. Practically it is superfluous to mention these small signal flutes as a separate type; technically they are exactly the same as the longer flutes, which are blown at the upper end, and from which they are only distinguished by their shorter length, which varies from 6—8 cm., the long sacred flutes being sometimes as long as 1.70 m. Moreover there are a number of transitional forms, which nearly fill in the gap between the two extremes. For the sake of expediency these latter forms have been classed with the group of long flutes (on the map represented by the symbol ◢).

and another flute, open at the upper extremity and semi-closed at the bottom with a pierced nodium, used by the Sabèri [27]) (east of the Apauwar river), are mentioned for the above regions only).

The two forms, generally used, of the Northcoast are described very minutely by VAN DER SANDE [28]). One of them, which is known in a number of sizes [29]), is thin in proportion to its length and is blown from the upper end (pl. XII, figs. 48—50). The lower extremity is closed by a nodium (the flute is "covered"). Consequently only the *uneven* aliquot-tones can be produced, besides the principal tone.

The other type, which also occurs in different varieties (figs. 38—46), is proportionally wider and shorter. This type is also closed at one extremity, but occasionally it has in the centre, as a rule however nearer to the closed end than to the open one — although this occur in very rare cases — a lateral (round, oval or square) hole, so that here the *even* aliquot-tones could also be produced, but for the fact, that the great diameter of the tube seems to preclude the production of more than one single tone [30]). These short, thick flutes are much easier to play, than the long thin ones [31]). These latter are so difficult to

---

27) Mus. Bat. Soc. No. 16361/2.

28) N. G. III p. 307.

29) Compare WIRZ I p. 75 note 55; V p. 331 a. f.

30) However, this does not always seem to be the theoretical groundtone. VAN DER SANDE (ps. 313/4) at any rate, gives in most cases a second tone, besides the groundtone.

31) Comp. JOSEPH SCHMIDT II ps. 53 and 56. He mentions two kinds of flutes of the Nor-Papuans, on the reef-islands off Dallmann-

handle, that no European player can draw a tone from them. My own efforts ended in ignominious failure. Only sturdy, broad-chested Papuans, in the prime of life, are able to do so. And Van der Sande [32]) tells us, that the blowing of these sacred instruments is so exhausting an exercise, that they can only keep it up for a short time and even then the performers are covered with perspiration from the exertion [33]): "I have seldom seen a Papuan exerting himself more, than in producing this sacred music". (Evidently the French "sacré" has not got its double meaning for nothing.)

About the position of the body, and the proper movements for playing, details have been given elsewhere [34]), and also about the meaning in social life of these instruments, which no woman must ever behold.

Of the five flute-records, which are numbered XI—XV inclusive, the numbers XI, XII (first and third fragment), XIII, XIV (first fragment) and XV show great similarity; they were taken from performances by the same players, using the same set of instruments. These latter belong to the long narrow type. The middle part of phon. XII, and also phon. XIV (second and third fragment) bear another char-

Note 31 (continued).
hafen: one short kind, styled *female*, which is easy to play, and a long type, styled *male*, the playing of which is very difficult.
32) N. G. III ps. 295/6.
33) Comp. also Bink p. 34, and Koning p. 11.
34) Compare Wirz I ps. 66/8, and V p. 333.

acter, not only as regards the tunes, but — partly at least — also as regards the nature of the instruments, among which are a few flutes of the short thick type with lateral blowing-hole.

The tones of this music have been measured as carefully and accurately as possible, with the intention of determining, which series of aliquot-tones are used. However, this effort failed, one of the reasons of this failure being the untheoretical height of these aliquot-tones. This descrepancy is mentioned already in Van der Sande's report [35]).

Already for the first of the flutes, described by him, the author gives for instance *C sharp* as groundtone; as its harmonics, however, *A*, *c* and *e*. This statement refers to a "covered" flute, so that in this case only uneven part-tones are to be considered. When starting from *C sharp* as groundtone, we find, however, $\dfrac{g\ sharp}{3}$, $\dfrac{e'sharp}{5}$, $\dfrac{b'}{7}$, $\dfrac{d''\ sharp}{9}$, $\dfrac{g''}{11}$, etc.

Now ought we to look upon *A*, *c* and *e* as — too low — 7th, 9th, and 11th part-tones? Or should we accept the possibility, advanced by prof. Von Hornbostel, that the groundtone is not *C sharp*, but *D*, so that *A*, *c* and *e* might be taken as 3rd, 7th and 9th part tone? But then, how are we to reconcile the one and the other to Van der Sande's remark, that the blowing is done with so much force, that the 2nd or 3rd harmonic dominates the groundtone? This seems to indicate, that there is no question of sounding the

---

35) N. G. III p. 313/4.

higher part-tones. (We must, however, remember, that the instruments are "covered", so that the words 2nd and 3rd part-tones are to be understood as 2nd and 3rd of the *uneveh* series, which means part-tones 3 and 5 from the theoretically complete series.)

We may take it, that, partly at least, the solution of these incongruities must be found in the manner of blowing. The performer on such a long thin flute does not touch the instrument with his lips; he holds the upper extremity of the flute with both hands, laying the thumbs along the cheeks, and he blows into his hands in the direction of the mouth-piece [36]. Practically the column of air, set vibrating by the blowing, is lengthened by an irregular piece formed by the hands of the player.

However this may be, the series of tones, occurring in these five phonograms, appear to be of a fairly irregular composition.

It is not worth while to make a score of this flute-music. The instruments are generally blown in a regular rhythm, let us say, crotchets or quavers; the tones are alternately stressed and unstressed:

---

36) ibid. p. 295 and plates 189, 191 and 192; Lorentz ps. 152 and 153; Koning p. 11: "The performer takes the mouthpiece of the flute between the balls of the hands, the thumb pointing upwards, and puts the instrument to his mouth in this manner". — Le Roux p. 484: "The flute is not put into the mouth, but the breath is blown through the tightly closed hands into the opening of the bamboo. Both thumbs are laid along the cheeks". — See also Wirz I p. 66.

Phonograms XI, XII (first and third fragment),
XIV (first fragment) and XV.

The tones produced are the following:

| I | 435 | II | 362 | III | 319 | IV | 165 | V |
| 46 | | 594 | | 732 | | 880 | | 968 |

In phon. XI, however, it is impossible to fix the
height of the tone IV with certainty, because of its
transient character (it seems a trifle higher than is
stated here), and tone V is missing altogether. Tone
III is also very vague. Tone I and II predominate,
especially the latter.

At one moment one gets the impression, that tones
II and III are produced by the same instrument;
at another one imagines, that III, IV, and V belong
together. But at least one of these suppositions must
be wrong, unless one assumes, that both flutes, the
records of which we have here, produce a perfectly
similar tone III; and this is hardly possible. The
other supposition, that in this phonogram we have
the record of only one instrument, must be rejected,
as it is customary always to play two flutes at
the same time; moreover, Mr. LE ROUX assured us,
that the phonograms were taken from two instruments.

The development of this record XI is the same as that of *phon. XII (first and third fragment)*.

This starts in slow times, on tone I, blown very softly. Then tones II and III are heard. The time has gradually become normal, viz. about 60 tones per minute [37]), and the sound strong up to *ff*. Then follows a swifter part of about 120 tones per minute. Here only tones III, IV, and V are used. Then there is a return to the original time and to the softly breathed tone I and the loud II with its satellite III. Strong crescendo. Again the swift second part with the higher tones and then again a return to the first part at the "normal" time.

Phon. XIII has apparently the same development as phons. XI and XII (first and third fragment), but in places it is not very clear. We may say the same of the beginning of *phons. XIV and XV*. About the latter record it may be mentioned, that tone II (sounding raw and harsh) predominates and is sometimes intoned a little higher than in the earlier records.

The middle part of phon. XII bears an entirely different character. The four tones of which it is composed have a sweet, soft, organ-like sound, and because they happen to form a, rather true, chord, viz. four tones of a none-chord, which sounds fami-

---

37) Compare also WIRZ I p. 67.

liar to Western ears, this part seems quite pleasant
to a European:

The time is also about 60 tones per minute.

To conclude with, we have *record XIV*. In this
phonogram we can distinguish two other parts besides
the first short fragment, of which we spoke above.
At first there is a sort of soft, indefinable tangle
of sounds, a melodious whispering, in the higher
tones, played very swiftly (time approximately 240
tones per minute). After that a plaintive movement,
repeated several times (bird-voices?) [38]), beginning
in a time of 148 tones per minute, more or less, in-
increasing to about 196 tones p.m. and then slowing
down again to 148 tones p.m. Its "tune" is:

Mr. Le Roux tells us, that, as far as he recollects,
these four notes were produced on four different
flutes, viz. two long ones and two short ones.

---

38) See before p. 7/8.

§ 3.

THE TRIBES OF THE NASSAU RANGE
(CENTRAL MOUNTAINS)

Although, as the crow flies, not more than 150 km. distant from the tribes of the Van Rees Mountains, and less than 50 km. from the tribes inhabiting the lake-plateau, who also know the sacred flutes mentioned before, the Papuans of the Nassau-Range, though they keep up bartering intercourse with those other tribes [39]), know no other musical instrument than the *jew's harp* (which seems to be found all over New-Guinea) [40]). But, what is still more remarkable, is the fact, that, as has been said in the introduction to this sketch, they possess, side by side with melodies of a most primitive character, much more elaborate melodies of an entirely different nature.

JONGEJANS [41]) has already given us some details about the singing of the Uringup, who inhabit the Swart Valley. These details, to which a number of his own observations are added, may be found again in WIRZ [42]).

---

39) WIRZ II ps. 5/6.
40) See the map. Compare also WIRZ II p. 120.
41) JONGEJANS p. 604.
42) WIRZ II p. 113 a.f.

The greater part of the melodic phrases, hitherto collected, are of that very primitive type, and their compass does not exceed a fourth, as a rule. They seem to remind us of our own nursery rhymes and ditties. As examples WIRZ gives:

and a fourth, taken from JONGEJANS:

But JONGEJANS noted down still another fragment, which is entirely different from all the others:

If we did not know any better, we might take it for a military signal. And this impression is strengthened by a number of melodies and fragments of melodies, which Mr. LE ROUX and his assistant MOHAMMED SALEH brought back from the Awèmbiak and Dèm tribes, who are closely related to the Uri-

---

43) This melody is sung by a chorus, against which the "precentor" sings a continuous c e c e.

44) The bars, placed after each group of three notes, were put by me; the author did not place them himself, but left a space.

ngup. It is a pity, that these melodies could not be recorded on wax cylinders, but only by ear: through particular circumstances, about which Mr. LE ROUX is sure to give some details in his report (which is to be published shortly), the phonographic apparatus was not included in the luggage, taken on the excursion to the central mountains. As a result of this omission we have to be content to work on second hand data. Luckily the excursion lasted long enough for the participants to learn to sing, without mistakes, the fairly simple songs of these mountain tribes, and to commit them to memory. But it is a well-known fact, that there is always a strong tendency "to correct" strange or unusual intervals and to put them in concordance with well-known intervals of one's own musical system, when there is only the musical memory to guide one [45]).

If we had no other data about the music of the Central tribes, there would be every reason to regard these melodies, at any rate as regards details, with a certain amount of distrust. However, since music of a very similar nature has been recorded, not only from these regions, but also from elsewhere in New Guinea and the adjacent countries, it is possible to test this music, by comparison with what had already been observed by others, and (partly) described at the hand of phonograms, — although the new material, on account of its *vilium originis*, is not fitted for the demonstration of eventual peculiar

---

45) Compare VON HORNBOSTEL VI ps. 5 and 6.

characteristics, by which this music should distinguish itself from that of those other regions. In short: the new material is to be trusted in so far as it is congruent with other Papuan music, but it deserves a certain amount of distrust, in so far as it shows characteristics, unknown from elswhere.

If the musical data, brought back by Mr. LE ROUX from the Nassau Range, do not enable us therefore to arrive at definite conclusions, they undoubtedly contain some very useful suggestions as to the direction in which further investigations should be continued.

The melodies, which could be noted down from Mr. LE ROUX's singing and whistling, on his return to Weltevreden, and from the violin performance of his assistant (both performances bearing each other out in details), are to be found in the Table II, hereafter.

What is the origin of this "fanfared", this "flourished triad"-music?

Our ignorance of the music of the adjacent tribes is the great obstacle in the way of solving this problem. Our failure in finding relationship in a certain direction would be by no means conclusive evidence that this relationship does not exist. But the few melodies and fragments of melodies, and the other rather meagre information we have been able to collect from the Northern regions, do not seem to point to the *probability* of finding any closely related music in those parts.

Neither is this to be expected from the Western districts, which, like the Western part of the North-coast, is fairly strongly under Malay influence [46]).

As regards the North I had at my disposal some observations made by VAN DER SANDE, and the melodies of the Sarmi people (near Humboldt Bay), published by Lieutenant GJELLERUP, A.M.C. [47]).

The latter are unmistakably partly of the "tiled" type, and therefore "Australian", f.i.:

and

46) Encyclopaedie van Ned.-Indië, vol. II ps. 834/5. In connect-ion with this are mentioned the island Misool together with the islands and the coast *east* of Cape d'Urville. This should certainly be *west* of that Cape, firstly because the only islands of any importance lie west of it, and secondly, because the influence of Tidore, which is meant here, could not very well be felt on the east side without showing itself on the west side in a much higher degree. The Encyclopaedia mentions from these regions the following instruments: *rebab*, *rebana* (= *terbang*), *gong*, and *tifa* (the Malay drum). VALENTIJN mentions just the same instruments (vol. I ps. 151/2, 155, 156, 160) as characteristic of the Moluccos, and especially of Ternate and Tidore. — The cylindrical drums (viz. pl. VI fig. 20 hereafter) of the coast districts west of Cape d'Urville, also show the Malay influence very distinctly in the way the skin is fastened. See further the map.

According to Prof. VON HORNBOSTEL some of the phonograms from Misool, taken by TAUERN and transcribed by HERZOG, and which are now in the Phonogram Archives in Berlin, also distinctly show Malay influence.

47) GJELLERUP II ps. 42, 43, 48, 49, and 50.

The examples given are at the same time specimens of "triad"-melodies, however without being "fanfared".

A single one goes a little further on the way to that "fanfared" music:

Others of GJELLERUP's melodies seem to betray Malay influences, like the following, rather melancholy, but melodious little song:

However, it would be too risky to draw conclusions from this material in view of the way in which the reproduction was obtained, viz. "Lieutenant KRUYT was kind enough to note down the melodies as well as he could under the circumstances. We are also indebted to Mr. BOUVY for further elaborating (sic!) the material provided by Mr. KRUYT." Grateful as we are for the trouble these gentlemen took for us, it is plain, that a notation, produced in the way mentioned, does not constitute a very trustworthy basis for a hypothesis.

Then there are the data about the Kauwerawèt, given in the preceeding pages.

29

Finally, at the Ethnographical Exhibition at Weltevreden in 1929 I had the opportunity of making records of the songs of various tribes from the North, namely the inhabitants of the island Japèn, of the Waropèn Coast and of Humboldt Bay. The songs of Japèn showed closed relationship with these of the Kauwerawèt: pure ''tiled'' music with all the characteristics mentioned above, f.i.:

The songs of the Humboldt Bay people were much more varied, but, for all that, they showed, as a whole, the same marks of relationship, and certainly no ''fanfared'' character. One instance may suffice:

Some of the songs of the Waropèn Coast, on the contrary, seem to have undergone Malay influence, as I am inclined to deduce from the ''pélog-character'' of some of those melodies, in which half-tone intervals often occur:

Other melodies showed a pronounced "triad"-character; these again however were not "fanfared".

If I remember well, no one of the melodies, I recorded, exceeded the limits of one octave, with one remarkable exception: a festal song from Sarmi (the village, where GJELLERUP got his melodies).

That beautiful and varied melody extends over no less than one octave and a fourth, and, therefore has the same compass as one of Mr. LE ROUX's Awèmbiak melodies (Table II mel. α) [48]).

Still less has come to light of the music of the tribes on the South Coast. The melodies, published by MYERS [49]) of the population of Torres Straits, are purily Australian; consequently their style is the same as that of the Kauwerawèt melodies, mentioned above. The few small fragments of the Marindeanim songs, recorded by KOCH [50]) and WIRZ [51]),

---

48) As the copies of the records under consideration, at the moment this treatise was finished, had not reached us from Berlin, where Prof. VON HORNBOSTEL was kind enough to make arrangements for the preparation of matrices, I could only insert the melodies I noted down, when recording them, and could only give a few particulars about the others (which, in general, have a more complicated structure and therefore could not be noted down on first hearing). When back in Java, those records will be transcribed and published soon.

49) MYERS ps. 244/7, 262, and 263.

50) KOCH II ps. 565 and 566.

51) WIRZ IV ps. 130 and 285.

show indeed a certain predilection for the third and occasionally a triad, so that they might be classed with the type of the short Dèm-melodies in Table II under ɩ — ϑ; but for all that they remain far removed from the lively fanfares of the songs, shown in that same table under α — δ:

(Koch II p. 565)

(Koch II p. 566)

(Wtrz IV p. 130)

(Wtrz IV p. 285)

Finally I noted down from the singing of a Kaoh-river man (Upper-Digul), who came to Bandoeng with Dr. DE ROOK, the following melody:

When, however, we turn our attention to the East, we find a very different state of affairs.

In 1910 the well-known ethnologist and R. C. missionary Father WILHELM SCHMIDT, S. V. D. gave a lecture in Vienna, on the occasion of the Con-

II. The blowingconch as a signalling-instrument: a Binandeli on the banks of the Mambare near the village of Sia.

gress of the International Association of Music, on the songs of the Karesau Papuans. Karesau — see the map — is a small island belonging to the Schouten Islands [52]) off the coast of the former German New-Guinea. Only a few miles separate this island from the mainland.

The characteristics of Karesau music, mentioned by Father SCHMIDT [53]), are:

I. *Subject matter*: 1. ritual songs; 2. popular songs.

II. *Form of the text*:

    1. special linguistic forms: a) nasalising; b) duplications;

    2. rhythm: alternation of stressed and unstressed syllables; as a rule a verse with three accents alternates with one of two accents;

    3. parallelism: the initial words of two lines are the same; the end-words are different;

    4. interrupting the rhythm of the verses in singing by the insertion of a ''stop-gap''-*o*. (SCHMIDT calls it: Flick-o.)

III. *Execution*:

    1. always with the accompaniment of drums or at least of knocking with the fingers;

---

52) The archipelago north of Geelvink Bay also is called Schouten Islands after that famous navigator.
53) SCHMIDT II ps. 297/8.

2. repeated tremolo (with the root of the tongue), especially in long drawn notes;

3. fioritura;

4. repeated transitional legato, by means of which the singer connects the end of one line with the beginning of the next without taking a new breath.

IV. *Tonal system and melodic structure*:

1. the pieces, formed of triads — very often exclusively so — always are of a ritual character;

2. in the others a pentatonic scale is used;

3. the course of the melodies is generally in the descending line;

4. the melody always ends on the lower keynote, or, starting from this note, it leaps on to its higher octave.

V. *The origin*:

1. the ritual hymns are, so it seems, handed down from generation to generation, or else they have been adopted from other tribes at the same time as the corresponding ceremonies;

2. folk-songs are being made and composed up to the present day.

Now, which of these characteristics do we find in the melodies brought back by Mr. LE ROUX?

Some of them are found in the songs of the Kauwerawèt (Table I) as f.i.:

II   sub 3: parallelism: f.i. mamàkànanè < kèrè-
            kànanè [54]);
IV   sub 2: the use of the pentatonic scale;
IV   sub 3: the descending movement of the melo-
            dies;
IV   sub 4: the lower key-note as final note.

As is the case with the Karesau-music, the characteristics, mentioned above, refer to the folk-songs
(I sub 2), which are still being invented at the present
day (V sub 2); see p. 12 of this treatise.

As regards the ritual songs of the Karesau (I sub 1),
no equivalent of these is found in the music of the
Mamberamo Papuans, nor in that of the population
of the coast; but, curiously enough, we *do* find this
equivalent in the songs of the Central tribes, the
latter being characterized (see Table II) by:

I sub 1: their *ritual* use;
II sub I b: *duplications*: melody α : soloe-soloe,
                          naga-naga, mi-
                          na-mina;
                melody β : naga-naga, dé-
                          ga-déga;
                melody δ: waé - waé - waé-
                          waé;
                melody ϑ: wé'oe'wé - wé'
                          oe'wé, wie'o -
                          wie'o;

54) Le Roux p. 308.

II sub 3: *parallelism*: melody β : naga-naga dé-
wi wowai, dé-
ga-déga doewa
wowai;

melody δ: jao awie o
jéwé awie o;

melody ε: oewa ie a
oewa jo a;

melody ζ: oewé a wé
oewé a kwa;

II sub 4: *interruption of the verse-rhythm by "stopgap"-
vowels* f.i.:

in melody β : by o, a, o;
in melody γ: by o, a, é.

WIRZ also draws attention to this peculiarity [55]).

III sub 1: *accompaniment* of the singing by snapping
or clicking the fingers;

III sub 2: *tremolo* with the root of the tongue in the
long drawn notes;

III sub 4: *interlinking* the lines of the text by peculiar sighs, produced by sucking in the
breath [56]);

IV sub I: *the melodies are built up of triads*.

As the Central tribes have other, simpler, worldly melodies — as was shown above — besides their
ritual chants, we find in the Nassau Range also the

55) N.G. XVI p. 116 (WIRZ II): "Die Worte werden beim Singen
nicht in üblicher Weise ausgesprochen, endigen vielmehr ştets auf
einen Vokal, was als erster, tastender Versuch einer Reimbildung auf
zu fassen ist. Auch der Melodie wegen pflegt man die Worte stets auf
einen Vokal auslaufen zu lassen."
56) Whilst the singer shuts his eyes in extasy.

peculiar phenomenon, which we might term "musical stratification". MYERS states, that he found the same peculiarity in the music of the Murray Islanders in Torres Straits [57]): he distinguishes as many as three strata. And according to what Father SCHMIDT tells us of the music of Karesau, the same may be said of that island [58]).

The texts, especially those of the ritual chants, are generally only half understood by the performers; they are full of obsolete, difformed or distorted words [59]).

It is not necessarily the age of the text only, which makes it (partly) unintelligible: transmigration may easily have played a part here, for shells, tobacco and

---

57) MYERS ps. 255/6.

58) As far as I know, nothing has come yet of the proposed publication of a great number of Karesau songs by Father SCHMIDT. The plans for this publication were mentioned in Anthropos II p. 1030.

59) The texts of the dance-music of the coast-population provide also instances. VAN DER SANDE says in this respect (N. G. III p. 308): .... "It is a very remarkable fact that the language of the songs, as well in Humboldt Bay as in the district of Seka and to the West, is said to be an ancient language, which is now no longer spoken and only imperfectly understood .... (MAC FARLANE) writes that the short sounds, sung in chorus, have no meaning; — perhaps the meaning has got lost, as suggested above. Similar particulars were gathered by MAC GREGOR and in Kaiser Wilhelmsland by SCHELLONG and PÖCH ...... The use of that old language enables the villagers, who ...... visit other villages, to join in the general song."

For British and former German New Guinea it is indeed the same thing over again: "Wie ein französischer Missionar aus English Neu-Guinea erzählte, ist es häufig, dass die natives die eignen altererbten Lieder nicht verstehen, da die Sprache sich mit der Zeit in den einzelnen Distrikten verändert hat. Dieselbe Beobachtung machte ich in Finschhafen........." (SCHMIDT-ERNSTHAUSEN p. 268). — See further also RECHE ps. 447/8, who quotes PÖCH extensively, and also PÖCH himself in PÖCH I ps. 232/3, and III p. 610.

stone hatchets were not the only things that were passed on from tribe to tribe.

Father SCHMIDT [60]) has been already cited in this respect with regard to Karesau and the adjacent regions. About Torres Straits MYERS says [61]): "They (viz. the songs of the Murray Islanders) .... show evidence of the great traffic in tunes, which may go on between the inhabitants of neighbouring islands, thus raising the general question as to how far the fundamental characteristics of the music of a given people are fixed or are modifiable, temporarily or permanently, by the importation of foreign airs." SCHMIDT-ERNSTHAUSEN mentions songs from Rook Island, which have been adopted by the Jabim of the opposite coast of New-Guinea (round Finsch Harbour) without the slightest understanding [62]); GUPPY speaks of a melody, which the inhabitants of Treasury Island (Mono) had appropriated from the Duke of York Island [63]); SELIGMANN mentions songs, which the Koita, round Port Moresby, adopted from the Motu [64]).

So the striking resemblance between the ritual chants of the Karesau Islanders and those of the pygmoid tribes of the Nassau Range *might* therefore easily find its origin in the handing on of these melodies from tribe to tribe. The distance bridged over in

---

60) SCHMIDT II p. 298.
61) MYERS p. 238.
62) SCHMIDT-ERNSTHAUSEN p. 268.
63) GUPPY p. 141.
64) SELIGMANN II p. 152.

this case is certainly considerable, but then we may assume, that some of the tribes between the two extremes possess the same kind of melodies. The cultural development of the Mountain tribes at least seems to be perfectly homogeneous [65].

But handing on the music from tribe to tribe is by no means the only possible manner in which it has found its way from one district to another, far remote from the first. There are some other possibilities, f.i.: the inhabitants of the Nassau Range and of Karesau may at one time or other have had intercourse with each other, when living in each other's neighbourhood. And a third possibility: that this "fanfared" music, which is found at present among tribes far removed from each other, points to the fact, that at one time there was a certain civilization, spread over a wider area, which at a later period, was immersed in waves of a newer culture. Expressed in terms of geology, we might say, that these scattered outcrops might be considered as originating from a sporadically appearing "diluvium" in a territory entirely covered for the rest by Melanesian and Australian "alluvial" deposits.

Before we can decide, which of these possibilities, advanced here, correspond with the reality, the following questions should be answered satisfactorily and conclusively:

    a.   Are these "fanfared" melodies known to occur among other tribes in or near New Guinea?

---

65) WIRZ II p. 4.

b.   To which race — c.q. cultural agent — must these "fanfared" melodies be attributed?

c.   Is it possible to find the cause for these melodies being what they are and not being otherwise?

The answer to the first question can be readily given now and in the affirmative: on Bougainville, belonging to the Solomon Islands, East of New Guinea, the same kind of melodies are found. A proof of this is given in the examples reproduced in Table III as melodies α and β, which have been taken from VON HORNBOSTEL's "Bemerkungen über einige Lieder aus Bougainville"[66]). They belong to the songs of the Kongara, a mountain-tribe, and were recorded in 1912 and '13 by the ethnologist E. FRIZZI [67]). The same kind of melody is heard furthermore in some of the songs of the Jabim (Finsch Harbour), and of the witchsongs of Central New Ireland (= New Mecklenburg); melodies γ [68]) and δ [69]) on Table III give examples of this.

---

66)   VON HORNBOSTEL IV p. 53 ff. — The music of the N. W. Solomons is, especially in the coastal districts, much richer and much more civilized, than that of the Nassau Range. It presents very remarkable instances of part singing, sometimes with rudimentary canonforms, and also of the simultaneous performance of panpipe-orchestras and vocalists. Whenever this part singing occurs in New Guinea, it is of a much more primitive nature; sometimes it occurs purily by accident, because the songs, sung by a single performer, or by a chorus, overlap when the performers sing in turn (KOCH II p. 566; PULLE p. 191; RAWLING p. 247/8; VAN DER SANDE p. 310; WILLIAMSON p. 216; WIRZ II p. 114; LE ROUX — verbal statements about the Awèmbiak and the Dèm tribes.)

67)   For the rest most of the melodies of the N. W. Solomons do not consist exclusively of triads (comp. Table III mel. α); but also when scales with more tones are used, the third, fourth and fifth intervals predominate.

68)   Taken from SCHMIDT-ERNSTHAUSEN p. 270 mel. IV.

69)   Taken from PEEKEL I p. 50. See also ABEL I p. 821.

But the resemblance is not only found in the melodies; it shows also in the texts, which possess the same peculiarities as the songs of Karesau and the Nassau Range. VON HORNBOSTEL mentions f.i.: a) duplications of words, b) the completion of the text of a melodic phrase by yodling (therefore by vocalising), when the line is too short. And then he points out some other peculiarities, which Father SCHMIDT does not mention, but which are found in the songs Mr. LE ROUX brought back from the Nassau Range, viz. c) the rhythmical variability of polysyllables, and d) the appearance of end-rhyme [70].

Of the first case he gives as an example the word *nairoé*, which is sometimes stressed on the *i*, sometimes on the *é*, and sometimes on the *o*. We find a parallel case in the songs of the Nassau Range, given in Table II, in the variable pronunciation of the word *ambagagé*, which in text α is scanned ambaga*gé*, but in melody β as *am*bagagé(-o). In melody α we find side by side *mi*na and mi*na*, and in melody ♂ a*jé* and a*jé*.

End-rhyme is also found in the songs of the mountain tribes, at any rate in melody α : *wowai - oedjiwi - ragiwi*. In melody β the effort at rhyme is more primitive, at least in the first instance, as here it is made by the "stop-gap"-*o*: *wowai o a o - ambagagé o*. But the second rhyme of melody β may again be considered as a real one: *asiloé-naga-naga doewang waé*.

From the above we may conclude that, if the

70) The texts of the Coast Papuans are said to have no end-rhyme. (VAN DER SANDE, p. 308).

occurrence of this "fanfared" music in the central mountains is to be attributed to migration, we have to consider in the first place an influence coming from the (north-)east. Before, however, pronouncing a definite opinion on the greater or smaller probability of migration from that direction, or even on migration in general, it will be necessary to investigate other existing possibilities first.

At the hand of a wealth of material Von Hornbostel has proved, that those songs of the tribes of the Central mountains, which, in their essential properties show so striking a resemblance to the songs of the population of Bougainville, are *instrumental* airs. [71]) He demonstrates furthermore, that the melodies of Bougainville probably have their origin in the panpipe, which is found there everywhere (generally forming small orchestras).

Now does this mean that such melodies, wherever they occur, were evolved from the panpipe-technique? Or does it mean, that wherever in Austronesia the panpipe is found, we also meet this "fanfared" music? It means neither the one, nor the other.

Whereas the panpipe is found in many islands of Melanesia, Micronesia and Polynesia [72]) (pl. XIII figs. 58 and 59, and pl. XII fig. 54), there are no traces of that "fanfared" music, as far as we

71) Von Hornbostel II ps. 468/9, 492/3, 499, and 503.
72) Compare Sachs III p. 50.

know, outside the N. W. Solomon-group and the adjacent part of the Bismarck Archipelago. As for New Guinea, the panpipe — not counting the few rare and degenerate specimens of the Kaiserin Augusta River and of the lower Markham River [73]) (pl. XII fig. 55 and pl. XIII fig. 56) — is restricted to the South Coast, from the d'Entrecasteaux Archipelago and the Bentley Bay as far as Merauke [74]) [75]) (pl. XIII fig. 57); the "fanfared" music, on the other hand, belongs, as far as we know, exclusively to Karesau and the Central Mountains. And so we see, that the panpipe-area and the "fanfared"

---

73) BEHRMANN p. 195; NEUHAUS vol. I ps. 383/4 and fig. 306 a/b; RECHE p. 425; WERNER p. 56. — The Kaiserin Augusta River has been, since times immemorial, the gate-way, through which successive civilizations and races have entered the country. "Fasst man die Resultate der Untersuchungen am Lebenden und am Schädelmaterial zusammen, so erhält man den Eindruck, dass sich über eine dunkelhäutige, breitschädlige, plumpgeformte und kleinwüchsige — vielleicht bereits aus mehreren Bestandteilen verschmolzene—pygmäenartige Rasse ein oder zwei andere gelagert haben, die sich durch hellere Färbung, lange und schmale Körperbau und grösseren Wuchs auszeichneten...... Die Eindringlinge scheinen sich hauptsächlich im Mündungsgebiet und am Mittellauf niedergelassen zu haben (vielleicht zu verschiedenen Zeiten)......'' (RECHE ps. 56/7). And, according to NEUHAUS, it is a fact, that the Laé Womba tribe, the people, living on the banks of the lower Markham River, that knows the panpipe — is of Melanesian origin (NEUHAUS l.c.).

74) d'Entrecasteaux Archipelago: DE CLERCQ and SCHMELTZ, table IV behind p. 244;

Bentley Bay : FINSCH II p. 122; IV ps. 528/9;
Eeat Cape : DE CLERCQ and SCHMELTZ as before;
South Cape : ibid.
China Straits : ibid.
Orangery Bay : ibid.
Naiabu (opposite Yule Island): D'ALBERTIS vol. I p. 395;
Fly River, Kiwai, Daudai, Moatta: D'ALBERTIS vol. I opposite p. 305;
BAGLIONI ps. 264/5 and figs. 15/16; BEAVER III p. 178; CHALMERS p. 120; DE CLERCQ and SCHMELTZ, as before; LACHMANN 10

musical area are by no means identical. But there is
nothing astonishing in this. A melodic system, which
is founded on the phenomenon of part-tones (caused
by ''overblowing''; German: ''überblasen''), is not
necessarily derived from the panpipe; the music,
drawn from other wind-instruments, as f.i. the common bamboo flute, may also lead to this kind of

---

Note 74 (continued).

(LANDTMANN); LANDTMANN p. 45 (fig.) and 47; THOMSON p. 120
(fig.);

Torres Straits : HADDON III 282;
Merauke : KOCH II p. 567; WIRZ III vol. I ps. 83/4 and pl.
XXV fig. 1.

Further find-places of the panpipe (partly ''raft-'', partly bundle-
pipes) in the neighbourhood of New Guinea:

Solomon Islands: BURGER p. 59; BUSCHAN I vol. I p. 90 fig. 118; II
vol. II p. 160 Table VIII, 170; Finsch IV p. 532; FRIZZI p. 50;
GUPPY ps. 141/2, 144/5; VON HORNBOSTEL II pp. 463/4, 472,
474, 488, 490/2, 497; MEYER and PARKINSON vol. I pl. 29;
PARKINSON III p. 237; RIBBE ps. 65, 83, 84, 85, 87, 134;
SACHS III Table 4 figs. 27 and 30; STEPHAN and GRAEBNER
ps. 129, 130, and 131;

New Ireland (Neu-Mecklenburg): BUSCHAN II vol. II ps. 126/7, 150;
FINSCH IV ps. 528/9; VON HORNBOSTEL I p. 351 ff.; MEYER Vol.
VIII behind p. 1059 Table III fig. 18; PARKINSON III p. 145;
SACHS III table 4 fig. 32; SCHELLONG I p. 83;

New Hannover : Völkerkunde-Museum Berlin (VON HORNBOSTEL);
New Britain (Neu-Pommern): PARINSON I fig. 19 opposite p. 122;
French Islands : Völkerkunde-Museum Leipzig (VON HORNBOSTEL);
Admiralties : FINSCH IV p. 529; GRAEBNER II p. 33; Völker-
kunde-Museum Vienna (VON HORNBOSTEL).

75) The panpipe, mentioned in SCHMIDT-ERNSTHAUSEN's article
on the music of German New Guinea (especially from Finsch Harbour),
and which is reproduced and described on ps. 272/3, is undoubtedly an
instrument from the Bismarck Archipelago. The number of pipes (14)
and the careful way in which it is made, with the stepped bindings,
so typical of New Ireland, are sufficient proof of this. Compare VON
HORNBOSTEL I the fig. opposite p. 352, and II p. 464; SACHS I p. 289b.
— This is not the only instrument, which the author places erroneously
at Finsch Harbour, but which actually comes from the Bismarck Archipelago: the peculiar ''rubbing''-instrument also, he describes, and
of which he gives a picture (p. 273/4), is only known from New Ireland.

melodies, also through "overblowing". On the other hand we may take it for granted, that such "fanfared" music can only arise in regions, where wind-instruments are played. And anywhere and everywhere, where such instruments are used, this kind of melody may grow out of the instrumental music, without any influence from elsewhere [76]).

Now, in Karesau we find flutes [77]), and, although the Awèmbiak an Dèm tribes do not know any flutes, they are part of the cultural possessions of the neighbouring tribes from the lake-plateau [78]).

There is another strong argument against the connection between the panpipe and the "fanfared" music of the Karesau and the mountain tribes. The panpipe, product of a high East Asiatic civilization [79]), in all probability did not make its appearance in the Southern Pacific until rather late, and simultaneously with the tribes, that came from the mainland of Asia and migrated toward the East [80]). In this manner the instrument found its

---

76) VON HORNBOSTEL has proved very convincingly, that the alpine yodel has grown out of the vocal imitation of Alphorn-melodies — that is to say, also a result of "overblowing".

77) SCHMIDT I p. 1039.

78) LE ROUX (verbal statements about the Turu tribe).

79) The very remarkable series of tones, derived from an old Chinese scalar system, have found their way as far as South America and Central Africa. Compare VON HORNBOSTEL IIa, IIb, and VII.

80) Compare SACHS III p. 49 etc. Prof. SACHS classifies the panpipe, as regards the simple form, with his third, the "Zweiklassen-Kultur"-stratum, which has spread over Melanesia, some parts of Polynesia, South- and Central America, and the S. W. part of North America (Mexico, Pueblos, California). The ,,double" form, which is not met with in New Guinea, but occurs in the Solomon Islands (compare BUSCHAN I vol. I p. 90 fig. 118; FRIZZI p. 50) he classifies with his 7th,

way to New Guinea, — perhaps circuitously over island-groups, east of New Guinea — but it always remained a foreign element there. On all occasions one gets the impression, that it has badly assimilated, and has remained everywhere, up to the present day, a degenerate alien. For this reason also it is difficult to believe, that it can really be the origin of the above mentioned melodies ; it is all the more difficult to believe — and this is the third argument — because in Karesau, as well as in the central mountains of New Guinea and of New Ireland, only the ritual chant finds its expression in this melodic form, as was pointed out before, but the panpipe fulfills nowhere in those regions the function of ritual or sacred instrument [81].

On the other hand this circumstance makes the relationship with the flute-music much more probable, as the flutes are generally used for ritual purposes. This is especially the case among the population of the lake-plateau and of the North Coast, as well in the Dutch, as in the former German territories.

Although it is possible, that such "fanfared" music arises independently in different regions, one is inclined to think in this case of a certain connection, as it is found among peoples, who are probably

Note 80 (continued).

the Polynesian-South-American stratum (SACHS III p. 79); finally the bundle-pipe he places in a still later, viz. the Indonesian-Melanesian stratum (SACHS III p. 109).

81)   Compare also SACHS III p. 51.

bound by a tie of rather near ethnological relationship, among tribes, who possess, what we might call
"a great common divisor", like the mountain-people
of Bougainville and the pygmoid tribes of the Nassau
Range.

Of course it is always more or less risky to draw
conclusions about cultural relations from material,
which, as a rule, is quite inadequate; it is especially
dangerous in this case, because there are so many
gaps between the known facts.

GRAEBNER's wise words should still be our guide:
"Feststellung und Vergleichung ähnlicher Erscheinungen in den verschiedenen Kukturprovinzen der
Erde ist stets ein Verdienst. Jeder Versuch hingegen,
solchen Erscheinungen in näheren Zusammenhang
zu bringen, ist, wenn auch hier und da instinctiv
richtig, ohne weitere Vorarbeit mehr oder weniger
spekulativ, die Erklärung der eine durch die andre
ein ungenügend begründeter Analogieschluss. Denn
nicht nur bleibt die Art des etwaigen Zusammen-
hanges dunkel, was für Beurteilung und Interpre-
tation der Erscheinung immerhin von Bedeutung
ist; bei der flächenhaften Art, wie uns die Kultur
der meisten Völker bisher bekannt ist, müsste die
Uebereinstimmung bis zur Identität gehen, um uns
sicher zu machen, dass wir es nicht doch mit völlig
heterogenen Erscheinungen zu tun haben" [82]).

But still, even when fully agreeing with this point
of view, there is no reason why one should not go on

[82]) GRAEBNER II p. 28.

trying to find such cultural links. Only, the work must be done on condition, that we maintain a critical attitude towards the results of our speculations and give them no greater value, than they deserve. They must be taken simply as a working hypothesis, which is to be abandoned the very moment when facts are brought to light with which they cannot be made to tally.

While keeping this principle rigidly before me, I venture to answer the second of the questions, I put before, viz.: "to which race — c.q. cultural agent — must these "fanfared" melodies be attributed?" In doing so, I refer to the third possibility, advanced here, namely, that these melodies — which, as has been said, have, up to the present, been found in the Nassau Range, in Central Bougainville, in New Ireland, and in Karesau — bear witness to the continuance of a primeval common substratum of culture, a primary civilization, which in most places has been supplanted and overlaid by younger cultural waves.

Being part of those cultural possessions, which all peoples are most tenacious in preserving, namely those old forms, connected with religious life, an ancient musical form — be it, as far as the Nassau Range is concerned, without the wind-instruments, from the technique of which it originated — has continued to exist, side by side with different and younger music [83]). Assuming this, it also explains, why,

---

[83] So MYERS found in Torres Strait Islands older ritual music side by side with unmistakably younger, more variable worldly music.

apart from a small islet off the North Coast of New Guinea, it was apparently only the central mountains of the larger islands (New Guinea, New Ireland, Bougainville — probably also those of New Britain), that preserved that ancient form up to the present: those regions were best protected against the invasion of foreign influences from oversea. Would it be permissible, to count that form among the cultural possessions, which lead WIRZ, in his study of the pygmoid population of the Swart Valley, to make the following statement [84]: "Sicher aber ist, dass wir hier in Zentral Neu Guinea sehr deutliche Spuren einer ältesten Kulturschicht Melanesiens und Australiens deutlich vor uns haben, welche GRAEBNER in seiner Kulturkreislehre als negritische bezeichnet"?

If we may answer in the affirmative, this Negrito civilization, although comparatively primitive, stands from a musical point of view on a higher level than the younger cultures, by which it has been pushed aside or overlaid: the "fanfared" melodies are musically more advanced than the Australian "tiled" melodies and than the majority of the other musical phenomena, encountered thus far in New Guinea. Then it is that same cultural superiority, by which those Central tribes, who have preserved the pygmoid-negrito characteristics rather purely, distinguish themselves also in other respects (ethics, attitude towards strangers, pig-breeding, agriculture) from the

---

84) WIRZ II p. 7.

population of the coast- and lowland-districts, among whom the admixture of Australian or Melanesian blood is much greater.

Bandoeng, June 16th., 1929.

MELODIES

TABLE I.

Melody α. (Phon. I, II, III, and VI.)

Melody β. (Phon. V, VII, and VIII).

En - tje ma - rie - rie - bo pie - ra - wa - rie - nie - o màk a tie bie-bie-dau.

A - na - mau kie-tau kie - ta   ta ra - mau sàb - a - ta boe-noe kie - ta.

En-tje bò-ja, bò-ja, ko-bo ra-mak ò so tom à ko- ja sa- toe.

ossia

Melody γ. (Phon. IV, and XVI).

ossia

TABLE II.

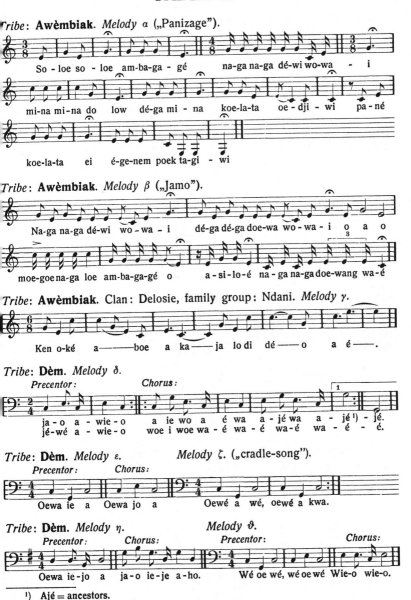

Tribe: **Awèmbiak**. *Melody* α („Panizage").

So - loe so - loe am-ba-ga - gé   na-ga na-ga dé-wi wo-wa - i

mi-na mi-na do   low   dé-ga mi - na   koe-la-ta   oe - dji - wi   pa - né

koe-la-ta   ei   é-ge-nem poek ta-gi - wi

Tribe: **Awèmbiak**. *Melody* β („Jamo").

Na-ga na-ga dé-wi wo - wa - i   dé-ga dé-ga doe-wa wo - wa - i   o   a   o

moe-goe na-ga loe am-ba-ga-gé o   a - si-lo-é na - ga na-ga doe-wang wa-é

Tribe: **Awèmbiak**. Clan: Delosie, family group: Ndani. *Melody* γ.

Ken o-ké   a———boe   a ka——ja lo di dé——o   a é——.

Tribe: **Dèm**. *Melody* δ.

Precentor: *Chorus*:

ja - o   a - wie - o   a ie wo a   é wa   a - jé wa   a - jé¹) - jé.
jé-wé a - wie - o   woe i woe wa - é wa - é wa-é   wa - é - é.

Tribe: **Dèm**. *Melody* ε.   *Melody* ζ. („cradle-song").

Precentor: *Chorus*:

Oewa ie a   Oewa jo a   Oewé a wé, oewé a kwa.

Tribe: **Dèm**. *Melody* η.   *Melody* ϑ.

Precentor: *Chorus*:   *Precentor*:   *Chorus*:

Oewa ie-jo a   ja-o ie-je a-ho.   Wé oe wé, wé oe wé Wie-o wie-o.

---

¹) Ajé = ancestors.

TABLE III.

Tribe: **Kongara** (South Bougainville). *Melody* a. [1]

Tribe: **Kongara**. *Melody* β. [2]

Tribe: **Jabim** (Finschhafen). *Melody* γ. [3]

Central New-Ireland (Neu-Mecklenburg). *Melody* δ. [4]

[1] Von Hornbostel IV p. 56 nr. 7.
[2]   ibid.   p. 55 nr. 5.
[3] Schmidt-Ernsthausen p. 270 nr. IV.
[4] Peekel I p. 50.

LIST OF INSTRUMENTS AND GUIDE
TO THE MAP.

Number of Sachs's cultural strata [*]	Symbol used on map	Name of the instrument	Literature
		A. Idiophones.	
10	⊟	cricket ("Galipnuss-Schnepper")	FINSCH IV 340 and Table XIX fig. 413; VON HORNBOSTEL II 484, 491; STEPHAN and GRAEBNER 123, 131, 173; WERNER 56.
	◠	scraper	SELIGMANN II 360 [**]).
3	▮	bamboo rasp (pl. III fig. 1)	HADDON III 270, fig. 226.
3	▯	rubbing-instrument made of bones	WOLLASTON II 270 [***]).
	╫	rattle made of a human skull	D'ALBERTIS vol. II fig. 14 fronting p. 378.
9	⧧	rattle made of split bamboo with a bundle of bamboo sticks inside (pl. III fig. 2)	HADDON III 273, fig. 232.
9	⦰	other basket rattles	Berlin Mus. nr. 10339; ROESICKE I.
1	✛	rattles made of dry fruits (pl. III figs. 3 and 4)	D'ALBERTIS vol. I figs. 20 and 31 fronting p. 305; BEAVER III 178; CHALMERS 120; DE CLERCQ and SCHMELTZ 104 and pl. XXVI fig. 7; Finsch IV 302, 544; FISCHER I 179;

[*] Compare p. 4 note 6.
[**] "................. from time to time making a rattling noise by rubbing their lime spatulae against the neck of their lime-gourds."
[***] "The Tapiro rub bones together to make a sqeaking noise."

Number of Sachs's cultural strata *)	Symbol used on map	Name of the instrument	Literature
1	✕	/	FUHRMANN 102; HADDON III 272/3; KRÄMER 53; LANDTMANN 47; MACLAY 322; Mus. Bat. Soc. nrs. 3147, 14780, 15860/3, and 18269; RECHE 424 and Table LXXXIV figs. 6 and 7; ROESICKE I; SCHMIDT-ERNSTHAUSEN 274; TAUERN 187; WERNER 56, 57, fig. 43 fronting p. 62.
		rattles made of shells (pl. III fig. 5)	BEAVER III 178; HADDON III 271/2; VAN DER SANDE 308 and pl. XVII fig. 1; SCHMELTZ I 243; SCHMIDT I 1035.
		rattles made of lobster pincers	Mus. Bat. Soc. nrs. 13663/4.
10	‡	sistrum for catching sharks	DE CLERCQ and SCHMELTZ 104; FINSCH IV 302; FISCHER I 179; SACHS III 103; TAUERN 41.
10	⊖	bell made of a Conus shell; usually the tongue consists of a boar's tusk (pl. III fig. 6)	Mus. Bat. Soc. nrs. 7059, 12697; VAN DER SANDE 107 and Table XVII fig. 7; STEPHAN and GRAEBNER 131 and Table II/III figs. 18, 19, and 20.
		bell made of a fruit	KRÄMER 54; KRÄMER-BANNOW 202 (fig.); STEPHAN and GRAEBNER 131 and Table II/III figs. 21, 22, and 24.

Number of Sachs's cultural strata *)	Symbol used on map	Name of the instrument	Literature
15	♂	bronze bell with a china tongue	Mus. Bat. Soc. nr. 14110.
19	♂	brass drum	Encycl. of N. I. vol. III 317b.
20	♂	gong	BURGER 30; VAN DISSEL I 917, II 1013, 1026; Encycl. of N. I. vol. II 835b; FEUILLETAU DE BRUYN 107; GOUDSWAARD 56; VAN HILLE 620, 622; VAN HOËVELL I 84; MARTIN 169; VAN DER ROEST 9, 12; SACHSE 98.
6	▲	slit-drum, usually made of wood; sometimes also of bamboo (pl. IV fig. 7) *)	BEHRMANN 165, 256, 280; BRANDES 329; BURGER 59; BUSCHAN I vol. I 112 (fig. 143); II vol. II 104 and fig. 76 on p. 108, ps. 126/7, 150, 158, 170; DE CLERCQ and SCHMELTZ Table IV behind p. 244; DETZNER 186; EBERLEIN 635 — 642 and fig. fronting p. 638; Encycl. of N. I. vol. II 835a; FINSCH II 13 = 31 = 50, and pl. XIII fig. 1; FINSCH IV 537/9; FRIE-DERICI I 101 a.f., 206; II 129; FRIZZI 49/50; FUHR-MANN 71; GRAEBNER I 299 a.f.; GUPPY 143; HAGEN 190; VON HORN-BOSTEL II 476, 491; KRÄ-MER 53, 54; KRÄMER-BANNOW 49 (fig.), 50, 51, 205, 215 (fig.), 216,

*) The red line on the map limits the slit-drum territory.

Number of Sachs's cultural strata *)	Symbol used on map	Name of the instrument	Literature
			217; Krieger 492/3; Luschan II 492/7 and figs. 31/5; Meyer vol. VIII behind p. 1059, Table IV fig. 9; Meyer and Parkinson vol. I pl. 16, 37, and 45; vol. II pl. 11 and 13; Neuhaus vol. I 231 (fig. 141), 259 (fig. 175), 316/7, 327 (fig. 225), 386; Parkinson I fig. 12 fronting p. 122; II 35, 40; III 78/80, 141, 144, 192, 237, 279, 328; Peekel II fig. fronting p. 1027; Pöch I 230, 236; IV 9; Reche 18, 440 a.f., 469, 471, 473, 476, 478, figs. 459/464, Tables LXXXVI, LXXXVII and figs. 2 and 3 on Table LXXXVIII; Ribbe 32, 88/9, 121, 133/4, 137 (fig.); Roesicke I; II 514; Sachs I 189 a/b; III Table 1 fig. 2, Table 2 fig. 21; Van der Sande 304/6; Schellong I 82/3; Schlaginhaufen 35; Schmidt III 77, 78, 80 a.f.; Joseph Schmidt I 707, 725; Stephan and Graebner 129; Vormann I 417; Werner 56, 245, 257.
3	⊔	hollow tree-trunk, used as a substitute for the slit-drum mentioned above	information by Von Hornbostel about Seran, Upper-Purari, and Marinde-anim.

Number of Sachs's cultural strata [*]	Symbol used on map	Name of the instrument	Literature
3	◬	sounding-block, ending in two points and with an oblong opening in the middle (pl. IV fig. 8)	Exploration-report 330; Mus. Bat. Soc. nr. 15932a; WASTERVAL 502; WIRZ I 67/8 and fig. 6 between ps. 2 and 3; V 335.
8	△	substitute for a drum, made of bamboo, with two incisions at one of the extremities (pl. IV fig. 9)	FINSCH III 122; IV 529, 534; KRIEGER 169; MURRAY fig. fronting p. 84 (?) and 100; PARKINSON I 128.
5	⊡	earth-drum, consisting of a board, to be trodden upon, laid over a pit in the earth	FINSCH III 31; IV 527; GRAEBNER II 33; GUPPY 144 (fig.); VON HORNBOSTEL II 492.
10	☐	xylophone with two keys („thigh''- and „tree-trunk''-xylophone) (pl. IV fig. 10)	BAMLER 500, 501; BUSCHAN II vol. II 126/7 and fig. 87 on p. 129; FINSCH III 28/9, 110; IV 534/5; KRÄMER -BANNOW 50 (fig.), 268; NEUHAUS vol. I 385/6; PARKINSON I fig. 20 fronting p. 20; III 80/1.
7	⚲	dancing-staves and -spears (pl. V fig. 11)	CHALMERS 120; Exploration-report 31; FINSCH III 31; IV 526; FISCHER II Table XXXIII figs. 1 and 1a, III 134/8 and Table XXIII; VON HORNBOSTEL II 482; KOCH II 600 and pl. IX nrs. 457/8; RECHE 420/4 and Table LXXXIV figs. 4 and 5, Table LXXXV figs. 1/7; RIBBE 88, 89

Number of Sachs's cultural strata *)	Symbol used on map	Name of the instrument	Literature
			(fig.), SCHMELTZ VI 215 a.f. and Table I — VI; SELIGMANN II 156; STEPHAN 30 (fig. 42) and 114 (fig. 96); STEPHAN and GRAEBNER I 120, 128; WIRZ VI 57 figs. 21 and 22.
7	♀	dancing-stave with sliding human skull	Exploration-report 327.
7	⊖	stamping-drum (pl. XIV fig. 11a)	BEHRMANN 195, 226 (fig.), 227 (fig.), 228; FINSCH IV 526; DE KOCK 159 (?); KRÄMER 53; MACLAY 323; PARKINSON III 289.
7	◑	water-stamping-drum	BRANDES 329; ROESICKE I; II 514.
3	●	percussion-sticks	BUSCHAN II vol. II 126/7, 177; FINSCH IV 526/7; PARKINSON III 81, 141, 289; STEPHAN and GRAEBNER 131.
5	⊕	beating-rod of bamboo (pl. V fig. 12)	NEUHAUS vol. I 384/5 and fig. 307; ROESICKE I.
3	○	bamboo-clappers (pl. V fig. 13)	FINSCH III 28; IV 526; HADDON III 270/1 (fig. 228); SCHMIDT-ERNSTHAUSEN 274.
	⊞	beaten Nautilus-shell	FINSCH IV 134.
	⊙	throwing-block (thunder-block) (pl. V fig. 14)	Exploration-report 330; Mus. Bat. Soc. nrs. 15933a/b, 18032; WASTERVAL 503, 505; WIRZ I 72 and fig. 7 between ps. 2 and 3; V 334.

Number of Sachs's cultural strata *)	Symbol used on map	Name of the instrument	Literature
10	☒	Jew's harp, made of wood, bamboo, palm-bark, glagah, or root (pl. V figs. 15 and 16)	D'ALBERTIS vol. I 395; BEAVER III 178; BIRO 58; BUSCHAN II vol. II 93 (pl. 60 fig. 8), 126/7; CHALMERS 120; DE CLERCQ and SCHMELTZ Table IV behind p. 244; Encycl. of N. I. vol. II 835a/b; vol. III 309a/b, 311a, 322a, 324a, 330b; FINSCH III 28, 122; IV 528, 529, 532; FRIZZI 50; GJELLERUP I 179; GOOSZEN 122; GUPPY 142; HADDON III 274/5; HAGEN 187; HOLMES 276; VON HORNBOSTEL II 491; J. J. S. 228; KEYSSER 25; LANDTMANN 47/8; LE ROUX (Kauwerawèt, Awèmbiak, Dèm; oral information); Mus. Bat. Soc. nrs. 6962, 14769a/b, 15149, 15620, 15215, 15928, 16215a/b, 16383, 16440, 16598, 19412a/c; PARKINSON I fig. 13 fronting p. 122; II 81/2; PULLE 190/1; RAWLING II 258/9, 274; REIBER 249; RIBBE 133; ROESICKE I; II 514; SACHS III Table 8 fig. 59; SACHSE 98; VAN DER SANDE 303/4, 312 and pl. XXVIII figs. 12/4; SAVILLE 310; SCHELLONG I 82; SCHMELTZ V 242, 243; SCHMIDT-ERNSTHAUSEN 274; STEPHAN and GRAEBNER 129 and fig.

Number of Sachs's cultural strata [*]	Symbol used on map	Name of the instrument	Literature
			132; STROEVE App. B p. 3; WILLIAMSON 212/4 and pl. 20 fronting p. 70, fig. 2; WIRZ I 67; II 120 and Table III fig. 11; III vol. I 84 and Table XXV fig. 2; WOLLASTON II 270.
8	⊢	rubbing-instrument, made of a block of wood with a smooth surface; it has two "undermined" parallel grooves, joined by a hole. The sound is produced by rubbing this block with the hand, which has previously been covered with resin or moistened with saliva (pl. V fig. 17)	BUSCHAN I vol. I 96 (fig. 125); II vol. II 93 (pl. 60 fig. 3) and 150; FINSCH IV 542; KRÄMER 56/8 and Table 14 and 15a; KRÄMER-BANNOW 240 (fig.), 279; PARKINSON III 145 and 146 (fig.); SACHS III Table 9 fig. 80; SCHELLONG 83; SCHMIDT-ERNSTHAUSEN 274.
5	■	sand-drum	WIRZ III vol. I 80 and fig. 3.

[Number of Sachs's cultural strata *)]	Symbol used on map	Name of the instrument	Literature
		B. Membranophones.	
13	⊞	drums in the shapes of vases, cups or goblets (pl. VI figs. 18, 19, and 20)	DE CLERCQ and SCHMELTZ 153/5 and pl. XXXIII nrs. 2, 4, 5, 6, 7, 8, 13, 14, 18; Exploration-report 329; VAN DER GOES 46 and pl. TT fig. 10; KOPSTEIN 50 (fig.); Mus. Bat. Soc. nrs. 6891, 7042/3, 18136; SACHS II 67 (fig. 44); Musicol. Archives Bandoeng; SCHMELTZ V 223; TILLEMA vol. IV 306 (fig.).
	⊟	bark-drum, covered with goatskin or bark	VAN DER GOES 125.
	■	cylindrical *) drum of wood, sometimes of bamboo. In the western districts under Malay influence, which is apparent in the manner of covering the drum, which is brought about by means of a rattan hoop and ties, with or without pegs (pl. VI VI figs. 21 and 22)	BEAVER III 178, 179, 180; BEHRMANN 226 (fig.); BUSCHAN II vol. II 91 a.f.; Encycl. of N. I. vol. II 833a; ERDWEG 302 and fig. 202; Exploration-report 329; FINSCH III 171; IV 534/7; VAN DER GOES 181; HADDON I 375; III 279/281; KRIEGER 330/1; Mus. Bat. Soc. nrs. 3143, 3265a/b, 6891, 12903/4, 15311, 15495, 16007, 18138 (?); VAN DER SANDE 312, 313 and pl. XXVIII figs. 8/11; SELIGMANN II 386,

---

*) Between the cylindrical and hour-glass shaped drums and between the cylindrical and the cup- or goblet-shaped drums there are transitional forms, of which it is difficult to say, whether they should be classed with the one group, or with the other.

Number of Sachs's cultural strata *)	Symbol used on map	Name of the instrument	Literature
			585, 588 and pl. LXIX fronting p. 586; Tauern 48, 75, 192.
	▯	two-legged drum (pl. VII fig. 23)	Mus. Bat. Soc. nr. 18033a.
	⊡	drum, about 8 feet in length, beaten with a wooden hammer	Beaver I 413; III 208.
10	⊠	hour-glass shaped drum, *) symmetrical or assymmetrical, with the posterior part cut off straight or ending in a fish's mouth, with or without a handle, and covered on one side with the skin of a leguan, varanus, kangaroo, buffalo, casuary, or snake. The skin is fastened by means of rattan or stuck down with some kind of glue (pl. VII figs. 24/6, pl. VIII fig. 27)	d'Albertis vol. II 269 (fig.); Beaver I 413, fig. fronting p. 411; III 178/9, 208, pl. fronting ps. 58 and 272; Behrmann 195, 227 (fig.); Brandes 275 (fig.), 311, 318 (fig.), 330 (fig.); Buschan I vol. I fig. fronting p. 73, 79 (fig. 101), 103 (fig. 134), 108 (fig. 139); II vol. II 91 a.f., pl. 60 fig. 2, ps. 126/7, 150; De Clercq and Schmeltz 151/6 and pl. XXXIII figs. 1, 3, 11, 12, and 20; Coenen pl. X nr. 2 fronting p. 20; Van Dissel I 956 fig. 10; Eberlein 635; Encycl. of N. I. vol. II 835a/b; Erdweg 303 and fig. 203; Exploration-report 329; Finsch II p. 13 = 31 = 50 and pl. XIII figs. 2/4; III 29, 31, 122, 171, pl. XXI fronting p. 142 fig. 1; IV 536, 537, 539; Fischer III 130/3 and pl. XXI figs. 7/10, pl.

*) See the note on the preceding page.

Number of Sachs's cultural strata *)	Symbol used on map	Name of the instrument	Literature
			XXII igs. 1/7; FRIEDE-RICI I 101 a.f.; FUHR-MANN 97/101; "Globus" XCII 20 a.f.; VAN DER GOES 163 and pl. VV fig. 3; GOOSZEN 123; GRAEB-NER II 42; "Graphic" 8 XI '30 p. 254; HADDON II 432 (fig.); III 278/281; HAGEN 185/6 and Table 43/5; HOLMES 91 (fig.), 275; HURLEY 172; KOCH I 391; II 598/600 and pl. IX nrs. 450/3; DE KOCK 164; KRÄMER 52/4; LE ROUX 485; LANDTMANN 43 a.f. (with a fig.), 452; LORENTZ fig. fronting p. 44; LUSCHAN I Table XXXI figs. 5, 7, and 8; MURRAY fig. fronting ps. 84, 92, and 100; Mus. Bat. Soc. nrs. 3196/7, 3243a/c, 3301, 6830, 6964, 6998, 10087, 10454, 13571/7, 13885, 14026, 14085/6, 14785, 14789, 14790/1, 14792a/b, 14793, 15310, 15313, 15930/1, 16276a/b, 16344, 16359, 16421, 18033b/c, 18135, 18137, 18139; Musicol. Archives Bandoeng; NEUHAUS vol. I 389, 394/5, figs. 309, 315/6; NEWTON 147 and fig. fronting p. 144; PARKINSON I fig. 21 fronting p. 122; II 40; III 80; PÖCH I 231 (fig. 1), 234, 235 (fig. 2), Ta-

Number of Sachs's cultural strata *)	Symbol used on map	Name of the instrument	Literature
			ble I fig. 4; II 397 figs. 2/3; III 615 (fig. 1); PRATT 51 and fig. fronting p. 40; RECHE 432/440, 478, figs. 447/458 and 475; REINHARDT Table 68 between ps. 480 and 481; SACHS III 111 and Table 10 figs. 85/6; VAN DER SANDE 304/6 and figs. 187, 188, and 190, pl. XXVIII figs. 1/7; SAVILLE 310, frontispiece and fig. fronting p. 212; SCHELLONG I 82/3; SCHMELTZ I 163 and pl. XV fig. 5; III 209; V 223 and pl. XI fig. 6 and XV fig. 2; VI 214/5; SELIGMANN I pl. XXIV fronting p. 332 fig. 1; II 360; SCHMIDT-ERNSTHAUSEN 271/2 and 273 fig. 1; JOSEPH SCHMIDT 725; SCHULTZE JENA Table XLIV fig. h; SELIGMANN II 161 and pl. XXIV fronting p. 161; STEPHAN and GRAEBNER 8, 129 and Table I figs. 22/3; THILENIUS II 329b/330a and 331 fig. 7; VERTENTEN 154/5 and Table XVIII figs. 1/2; VORMANN II 908; WERNER 56, 275, fig. 50 fronting p. 70; WILLIAMS I fig. between ps. 42 and 43; WILLIAMSON 212/3 and pl. 75 fronting p. 250 fig.

Number of Sachs's cultural strata *)	Symbol used on map	Name of the instrument	Literature
			3; WIRZ III vol. I 83/4, Table VI fig. 2 and Table XXV figs. 5 and 6; vol. II Table XV; IV 23 a.f., 26 a.f., 60, 90, 106, 112, 117 a.f., 121 a.f., 128, 130, 131, 134, 149, 179, 275, 279, 308, 310, 313, 376, fig. 28 fronting p. 96, 31 fronting p. 97, 36 fronting p. 128, 41 fronting p. 145, 57 fronting 193, 88 fronting p. 288, and 101 fronting p. 321; VI fig. 40; WOLLASTON I 141, 142 and pl. fronting p. 142 figs. 5/7.
	▢	drums (no details given, or insufficiently described or only mentioned in general terms)	D'ALBERTIS vol. I 395; BEAVER III 228; BINK 32; VAN BALEN 8; BAMLER 501, 511; BOREEL 234; BURGER 30; CHALMERS 120; DE CLERCQ and SCHMELTZ Table IV behind p. 244; VAN DISSEL I 971; II 1026; Encycl. of N. I. vol. II 835a/b; vol. III 307b/8a, 314b, 317b, 318a, 320a, 320b, 322a, 324, 327b, 328a/b, 331a, 332b, 333b; Exploration-report 329; FEUILLETAU DE BRUYN 40, 99, 107; FINSCH I 116; FRAZER 221, 226; "Globus" XCVIII 367; VAN DER GOES 46, 114; GOOSZEN 121/3, 125; GOUDSWAARD 56; VAN

Number of Sachs's cultural strata *)	Symbol used on map	Name of the instrument	Literature
			HoËvell I 85; II 128; III 173; Horst 28, 34; Hurley 148; J. J. S. 228; Keysser 25; Kirschbaum 204; Krieger 424; Maclay 323; Martin 169; Pöch V 153; Rawling I 247/8; II 59/61 and 281; Roesicke II 514; Van der Roest 4, 9, 12; Sachse 96, 98; Schmidt I 1042, 1048, 1055; Joseph Schmidt I 707; II 49; Seligmann and Mersch Strong 229; Stroeve App. B p. 3; Thomson 120; Vormann I 411, 417; Wasterval 503, 504; Wirz I 7, 67; V 268, 325.
17	◉	rebana ("Rahmentrommel")	Encycl. of N. I. vol. II 835a/b; Sachs II 64 (fig. 40) and 65; Sachse 98; Tauern 48, 75, 192.
10	▲	mirliton	Guppy 142/3.

Number of Sachs's cultural strata *)	Symbol used on map	Name of the instrument	Literature
		C. Chordophones.	
6	▲	zither made of the nerve of a sago palmleaf ("Stammseitiger Musikbogen") (pl. VIII fig. 28)	FINSCH IV 542; LANDTMANN 48; NEUHAUS vol. I 385, 386, fig. 308; RECHE 447; ROESICKE II 514; SCHLAGINHAUFEN 36.
6	●	musical bow, with one or two strings (pl. VIII fig. 29)	BEAVER III 178; BUSCHAN II vol. II 126/7; FINSCH III 29/30, 112; IV 542; GUPPY 142; VON HORNBOSTEL II 491; MEYER and PARKINSON vol. II pl. 23 fig. 2; PARKINSON III 82; Ethnogr. Mus. Cologne nr. 13761; WIRZ III vol. I 84.
18	■	bamboo idiochord ("Stammseitige Rohrenzither")	VAN HILLE 621.
22	♀	rebab	Encycl. of N.I. vol. II 834b/5a.
	♂	monochord (board with one chord and two bridges) (pl. VIII fig. 30)	BUSCHAN II vol. II 93 pl. 60 (fig. 6); FINSCH IV 542.

Number of Sachs's cultural strata (*)	Symbol used on map	Name of the instrument	Literature
		D. Aerophones.	
4	♂	wooden trumpet with blowing-hole at one extremity (pl. IX figs. 31 and 32)	CHINNERY 74 fig. 5; Exploration-report 330; FUHRMANN 96; HADDON IV 78; Mus. Bat. Soc. nrs. 14778a/b, 14779, 14781, 14794/7, 15314, 15712/3, 18281; Ethnogr. Museum Leiden, series 1482 nr. 1; WOLLASTON II 143.
9	●	wooden trumpet with lateral blowing-hole (pl. IX fig. 33)	BEAVER II 23; BEHRMANN 347 (fig.); CHINNERY figs. 1 and 2 fronting p. 73; FINSCH IV 532; FUHRMANN 103; GJELLERUP I 179; LUSCHAN III 111 fig. 20; Mus. Bat. Soc. nrs. 18023b, 18062; NEUHAUS vol. I 315, 384, fig. 215; RECHE 18, 430/2, figs. 442/6, Table LXXXVIII fig. 1; VAN DER SANDE pl. XXIX fig. 6; SCHLAGINHAUFEN 35/6 and fig. C2 and E2; SELIGMANN III 22 a.f.
	♂	wooden trumpet (no details given)	CHIGNELL 332; VAN EERDE 930; Encycl. of N.I. vol.II 834a/band 835b; vol. III 300b; ROESICKE II 514.
4	■	bamboo trumpet, with blowing-hole at one of the extremities (pl. IX fig. 34); sometimes it has a cocoanut as mouthpiece	BEAVER II 24; CHINNERY fig. 3 fronting p. 73; Encycl. of N. I. vol. II 835b; FINSCH IV 531, 534; FISHER III 133/4 and pl. XXII figs. 8/12;

Number of Sachs's cultural strata *)	Symbol used on map	Name of the instrument	Literature
			VON HORNBOSTEL II 490, 498; MACLAY 321/2; Mus. Bat. Soc. nrs. 16233, 16348, 16361/2; RECHE 426/7, fig. 435; RIBBE 134/5 (fig.); WOLLASTON I 143.
7	♂	trumpet made of a gourd (in New Britain with three finger-holes)	FINSCH IV 325; HAGEN 189; MACLAY 321; WERNER 56.
4	♀	conch-trumpet, with the blowing-hole at the apex; generally the instrument is made of a Triton shell (pl. IX fig. 35)	FINSCH III 27, 122, 254; IV 134; Mus. Bat. Soc. nrs. 7044, 8957, 15929a/b, 16432b/e; VAN DER SANDE 307/8, 314, pl. XXIX fig. 24.
7	♀	conch-trumpet, with a lateral blowing-hole; the instrument is sometimes made of a Fusus or Cassis shell, but generally of a Strombus (pl. IX fig. 36)	BUSCHAN II vol. II 158; CHINNERY 73 and fig. 4 fronting p. 73, 74 fig. 6; DE CLERCQ and SCHMELTZ pl. XXXIX fig. 3; FINSCH IV 133; GUPPY 143; HADDON III 283 and fig. 248; LANDTMANN 47, 452; MACLAY 324; Mus. Bat. Soc. nrs. 3122, 3261, 6997, 8998, 16432a; NEUHAUS vol. I 314; VAN DER SANDE 307/8, 314, pl. XXIX fig. 22; SCHELLONG 82b; WERNER 57, 257, fig. 38, fig. 11 fronting p. 57.
	♀	conch-trumpet, (no details given, or with an incomplete description or only mentioned in general terms)	BEAVER III 178, 208; CHALMERS 120; Encycl. of N. I. vol. II 834a/b,

Number of Sachs's cultural strata *)	Symbol used on map	Name of the instrument	Literature
			835a, vol. III 320b; Exploration-report 330; FISCHER III 129; VAN DER GOES 46, 125; GOOSZEN 122; GOUDSWAARD 56; HAGEN 190; VAN HASSELT 26; HOLMES 275; VON HORNBOSTEL II 484; KRIEGER 331; LEHNER 406, 408; NEUHAUS vol. I 384; RIBBE 135; VAN DER ROEST 9, 11; SCHMELTZ I 243; SCHMIDT-ERNSTHAUSEN 274; STEPHAN and GRAEBNER 131; WILLIAMS III 38.
7	▲	ocarina, made of wood or of a small cocoanut (pl. X fig. 37)	FINSCH III 28, 254; IV 302, 325, Table XIX fig. 428; HADDON III 281/2; HAGEN 189; MACLAY 322; Mus. Bat. Soc. nrs. 3262, 13661; RECHE 428/30, fig. 441; VAN DER SANDE 306; SCHMELTZ I 163/4; III 209; V 224 and pl. XI fig. 9/10c; SELIGMANN and MERSH STRONG 229; WERNER 56, pl. 38 fronting p. 57 fig. 6; WIRZ III vol. I 84 and Table XXV figs. 3/4.
9	△	buzzing-nut	BUSCHAN II vol. II 126/7; FINSCH IV 528; VON HORNBOSTEL II 483; SCHMELTZ IV 224.

Number of Sachs's cultural strata [*]	Symbol used on map	Name of the instrument	Literature
9		flute, closed at the top, open at the bottom, lateral blowing-whole (pl. X figs. 38/42; pl. XI figs. 43/46)	D'ALBERTIS vol. II pl. fronting p. 378 fig. 18 (?); BEHRMANN 129, 195, 221; BINK 34; Encycl. of N. I. vol. II 835a; vol. III 322a (?); Exploration-report 330; GJELLERUP I 179, 181/2 (?); J. J. S. 226; LACHMANN 12; LE ROUX 484/5; Mus. Bat. Soc. nrs. 3244a/b, 12908/9, 15567, 15568a/c, 15620, 15716, 15936a/b, 18023a/b, 18061a/b, 18117a/b; NEUHAUS vol. I 384; RECHE 349, 425/8, figs. 436/7; ROESICKE I (see LACHMANN); VAN DER SANDE 294/7, 306/7, 313/4, and pl. XXIX figs. 2, 6, 8, 9, 11, 13, 14, and 20; STROEVE App. B p. 3 (?); WIRZ V 331/5; VI 59 a.f. and fig. 129.
9		flute, open on either side, with lateral blowing-hole in the middle (pl. XI fig. 47)	DE CLERCQ and SCHMELTZ Table XXXIX nr. 10, and p. 157; WIRZ III vol. I 84.
9		flute with lateral blowing-hole and one finger-hole	HAGEN 186.
		flute, open at the top, closed at the bottom, no finger-holes, blown at the top (pl. XII figs. 48/50)	BINK 34; DE CLERCQ and SCHMELTZ 156/7; Encycl. of N. I. vol. II 835a; Exploration-report 330; FINSCH IV 530; GJELLERUP 179, 181/2 (?); VAN

Number of Sachs's cultural strata *)	Symbol used on map	Name of the instrument	Literature
			DER GOES 100, 178/9; HOLMES 276; LE ROUX 484/5 and oral information about the Boromesso, the Turu, and Batavia-bivak; LORENTZ 38/44, 152/3, 310; Mus. Bat. Soc. nrs. 7097a/b, 12905/7, 14023, 15714a/c, 15935, 15936c, 16066/7, 16068a/c, 16069, 16070, 16103/4, 16132/3, 16162, 16187, 16218, 16360, 18025h, 18059b, 18060a/i; VAN DER SANDE 295/6, 306/7, 313, figs. 189, 191, 192, and pl. XXIX figs. 1, 3, 7, 10, 12, 15/19, and 21; T.A.G. XXXII 663; WIRZ I 66/8, 70, 72, 73, 75/6, 78, 80; V 267, 324/5, 331/5, pl. XXXI fig. 27, VI fig. 98.
	▯	flute, open at the top, closed at the bottom, one finger-hole, and blown at the top	BAMLER 501 (?); FINSCH III 27; IV 530; SCHMIDT-ERNSTHAUSEN 272; HOLMES 276.
	▬	flute, open at the top, closed at the bottom, two fingerholes, and blown at the top	BAMLER 501 (?), BUSCHAN II vol. II 126/7; FINSCH III 27; IV 529, 530; PARKINSON I fig. 11 fronting p. 122; III 81; SACHS III Table 8 fig. 6 (?); SCHMIDT-ERNSTHAUSEN 272 and 273 (fig. 3).

Number of Sachs's cultural strata*)	Symbol used on map	Name of the instrument	Literature
	◤	flute, open at the top, the nodium at the bottom pierced, no finger-holes, and blown at the top	Exploration-report 330; FINSCH IV 530 (?); Mus. Bat. Soc. nrs. 13874, 13876, 13877 (?), 16361/2, 16461; REIBER 248.
	▬	flute, open at the top, the nodium at the bottom pierced, two finger-holes, and blown at the top	FINSCH IV 529, 530; HADDON III 283; SAVILLE 310; TISSOT 83 (pl. VI), 89; WILLIAMSON 212, 214/5.
	◩	flute, open at the top, three finger-holes, and blown at the top	FINSCH IV 532.
	▫	flute with a pierced nodium at either side, no finger-holes, and blown at the top	MACLAY 323; Mus. Bat. Soc. nr. 13875.
	⊓	very short flute, closed at the bottom by a nodium, and blown at the top	Exploration-report 330; GOOSZEN 122; Mus. Bat. Gen. nr. 18059a; VAN DER SANDE pl. XXIX figs. 4/5; SCHMELTZ V 243; WIRZ III vol. I 83/4.
3	■	double flute	BUSCHAN II vol. II 127; FINSCH III 27; IV 530.
11	⊞	nose-flute (pl. XII figs. 51/2)	FINSCH IV 528/9; FRIEDERICI I 104; LUSCHAN I 71 a.f.; TISSOT 89, fig. fronting p. 83, pl. VI.

Number of Sachs's cultural strata *)	Symbol used on map	Name of the instrument	Literature
	■	flute, consisting of more than one internodium, closed at the top, no finger-holes, with lateral blowing-hole	Encycl. of N. I. vol. III 331a; LACHMANN 12 (ROESICKE); RECHE 428, 429 (fig. 437).
10	◪	piston-flute, blown at the top, no finger-holes	BAMLER 501; ERDWEG 295; KRIEGER 169; NEUHAUS vol. I 384; SCHELLONG I 82; SCHMIDT-ERNSTHAUSEN 272, 273 (fig. 2).
	◪	water-flute	BUSCHAN II vol. II 92, 141; ERDWEG 295 and fig. 201; PARKINSON III 294/5.
6	☒	pan-pipe (single row) (pl. XII figs. 54/5; pl. XIII figs. 56/7)	D'ALBERTIS vol. I fig. fronting p. 305, 395; BAGLIONI 264/5, figs. 15, 16, 19, and 20; BUSCHAN II vol. II 127; Encycl. of N. I. vol. II 835b; · FINSCH III 122 and Table V fig. 4; IV 528/9, 530, 532; HADDON III 282; VON HORNBOSTEL I 351 a.f.; II 474 and Table XIII fig. 150; KOCH II 567; LACHMANN 10 (LANDTMANN); LANDTMANN 45 (fig.) and 47; MEYER vol. VIII Table III fig. 18 behind p. 1059; NEUHAUS vol. I 383, 384, figs. 306a/b; PARKINSON I fig. 19 fronting p. 122; III 145, 237/8; RECHE 425;

Number of Sachs's cultural strata *)	Symbol used on map	Name of the instrument	Literature
			SACHS I 289b; III Table 4 figs. 30 and 32; SCHELLONG I 83; SCHMIDT-ERNSTHAUSEN 272 and 273 (fig. 4); STEPHAN and GRAEBNER 129, 130, 131; THOMSON 120 (fig.); WIRZ III vol. I 84 and pl. XXV fig. 1.
7	⚐	pan-pipe (double row) (pl. XIII fig. 58)	BUSCHAN I vol. I 90 (fig. 118); II vol. II 160, pl. VIII, 170; FRIZZI 50; GUPPY 141/5; VON HORNBOSTEL II 463 a.f., 472 a.f., 490, 491, 495, 497/8, Table XIII fig. 149; MEYER and PARKINSON vol. I pl. 29; RIBBE 65 (compare 84), 83 (fig.), 48 (fig.), 85 (fig.), 87, 134; SACHS III Table 4 fig. 27.
	⚑	pan-pipe (no details given)	BEAVER III 178; CHALMERS 120; DE CLERCQ and SCHMELTZ Table IV behind p. 244; FINSCH III 28; GRAEBNER II 33; ROESICKE II 514; THURNWALD III vol. I 282/3, 461, vol. II 7/8; WERNER 56.
10	☊	bundle-pipe (pl. XIII fig. 59)	BAGLIONI 264/5, fig. 18; BURGER 59; FINSCH IV 529; VON HORNBOSTEL II 474 a.f. and Table XIII fig. 151.

Number of Sachs's cultural strata [*]	Symbol used on map	Name of the instrument	Literature
	☐	flutes (no details given, or insufficiently described or only mentioned in general terms)	D'ALBERTIS vol. II fig. 18 fronting p. 378; BEAVER III 178; BURGER 30; BUSCHAN II vol. 30; CHALMERS 120; DE CLERCQ and SCHMELTZ Table IV behind p. 244; VAN DISSEL II 1026; VAN EERDE 930; Explorationreport 329; Encycl. of N. I. vol. II 835b; FINSCH III 171, 254; IV 528; FRASER 221, 226, 233, 252; GOOSZEN 122; HAGEN 186, 189; VAN HASSELT 126/7; HORST 26/7, 34, 149; J. J. S. 228; KEYSSER 25; KIRSCHBAUM 204; TEN KLOOSTER 13; KONING 10/11; KRIEGER 330/1, 424; LANDTMANN 47; LEHNER 405; MEYER and PARKINSON vol. II pl. 23 fig. 1; NEUHAUS vol. I 384; PARKINSON II 35; SCHMELTZ V 243; SCHMIDT I 1039; JOSEPH SCHMIDT II 53, 56, 60, 62; STEPHAN and GRAEBNER 131; TAUERN 48; THURNWALD I 12, 27; VORMANN I 419, 426/7; WASTERVAL 502, 505; WERNER 56, 257; WIRZ V 352/3; VI 59 a.f.
	○	shawm, with one finger-hole	SCHELLONG I 82 [*]).

[*] "Von den beiden verschiedenen im Gebrauch befindlichen Flöten (sic!) ist die eine (*augagung*) nach dem Prinzip unseren Schalmeien construirt, mit nur einem Schalloch."

Number of Sachs's cultural strata [*]	Symbol used on map	Name of the instrument	Literature
3	☉	small shawm, made of a folded grass blade (,,Blättelinstrument'') (pl. XIII fig. 60)	HADDON III 283; HOLMES 276; REIBER 248; SCHMIDT I 1041; STEPHAN and GRAEBNER 124/5, 131, 173.
10	●	shawm, made of a very thin bamboo, the upper end of which is split, and serves as tongue (,,Blasspaltrohr'')	HADDON III 283.
9	⊖	burst blowing bamboo	FINSCH IV 529.
2	+	bullroarer (,,Schwirrholz'', ,,snorrebot'') (pl. XIII fig. 61)	BAMLER 494/8, 512; BEAVER III 185; BEHRMANN 195, 221; BUSCHAN II vol. II 126/7, 141; DE CLERCQ and SCHMELTZ 238/9, 241, and Table IV behind p. 244; DETZNER 190/1; Exploration-report 330; FINSCH II Table V figs. 5/6; III 35, 65; FRAZER 243, 249, 250, 255, 260, 261, 263, 291, 301, 302; FRIEDERICI I 102; HADDON II 418, 420 (fig.), 421; III 275/8; HAGEN 188/9; HOLMES 82, 84 (fig.), 127; VON HORNBOSTEL II 483/4; HURLEY 270/1; KEYSSER 36; TEN KLOOSTER 13; KRÄMER 56; KRÄMER-BANNOW 269, 270; KRIEGER 168/9; LANDTMANN 75 a.f., 403 a.f.; LEHNER 406/7, 408, 409, 410/414; Mus. Bat. Soc. nrs.

Number of Sachs's cultural strata *)	Symbol used on map	Name of the instrument	Literature
			16064a/b, 16065, 16102, 16131a/b, 17076, 18615a/b; NEUHAUS vol. I 259 fig. 173h, 385; vol. III 411 figs. 1/3, 412 figs. 5/9; PARKINSON III 82, 294, 301; PEEKEL II 1036 a.f.; PÖCH III 616; RECHE 349/351, 426, figs. 384/5 and Table LXV fig. 1; SACHS I 341b; VAN DER SANDE 306; SCHELLONG I 82; II 145 a.f.; SCHMELTZ II 12/20; STEPHAN and GRAEBNER 119, 131, and 119 fig. 124; THILENIUS II 332 b; WERNER 56; WILLIAMS II 165/171 and fig. fronting p. 165; WINTHUIS p. 83 a.f.; WIRZ IV 71, 141, 183, 283, 285 a.f.; V 350, 351/2, 352/3, 353.
	‡	whip-instrument (pl. XIII fig. 64)	HADDON III 274/5.
	‡‡	humming-top	FINSCH IV 325; STEPHAN and GRAEBNER 112 fig. 118 nr. 2.

Number of the plate	Number of the instrument	Name of the instrument	Origin of the instrument
		A. Idiophones.	
III	1.	bamboo-rasp (HADDON III p. 270 fig. 226)	Murray-island (Torres Straits)
	2.	bamboo-rattle (HADDON III p. 273 fig. 232)	ibid.
	3.	rattle made of dry fruits (Mus. Bat. Soc. nr. 14780)	Miku (affluent of the Digul-river)
	4.	rattle made of dry fruits (Mus. Bat. Soc. nr. 18269)	Lake Sentani
	5.	rattle made of shells (VAN DER SANDE pl. XVII fig. 1)	Humboldt Bay
	6.	bell made of a Conus-shell; the tongue consists of a boar's tusk (Mus. Bat. Soc. nr. 7059)	Humboldt Bay
IV	7.	slit-drum (SACHS III pl. 2 fig. 21)	Kais. Augusta - river
	8.	sounding-block (WIRZ I fig. 6 between ps. 2 and 3)	Humboldt Bay
	9.	substitute for a drum, made of bamboo (MURRAY, fig. fronting p. 100)	Port Moresby
	10.	xylophone with two keys (BUSCHAN II vol. II p. 129 fig. 87)	Gazelle-peninsula (Nw. Britain)
V	11.	dancing-stave (FISCHER II pl. XXXIII fig. 1)	Southern part of Princess Marianne-strait
XIV	11a.	stamping-drum (BEHRMANN p. 227)	Kais. Augusta-river
V	12.	beating-rod of bamboo (NEUHAUS vol. I p. 385 fig. 307)	Lower Markham-river

Number of the plate	Number of the instrument	Name of the instrument	Origin of the instrument
	13.	bamboo-clappers (HADDON III p. 271 fig. 228)	Murray-island (Torres Straits)
	14.	throwing-block (thunder-block) (Mus. Bat. Soc. nr. 18032)	Humboldt Bay
	15.	Jew's harp made of palm-bark (Mus. Bat. Soc. nr. 15928)	Humboldt Bay
	16.	Jew's harp made of bamboo (Mus. Bat. Soc. nr. 16215)	Sarmi
	17.	rubbing-instrument (BUSCHAN II vol. II p. 93 pl. 60 fig. 3)	Northern New - Ireland

B. Membranophones.

VI	18.	drum in the shape of a vase (Musicol. Archives Bandoeng)	Waropèn-coast
	19.	id. (Mus. Bat. Soc. nr. 18136)	Island Japèn
	20.	transitional form between vase-shaped and cylindrical drum (Mus. Bat. Soc. nr. 6891)	Waropèn-coast
	21.	bamboo-drum (Mus. Bat. Soc. nr. 12904)	Humboldt Bay
	22.	transitional form between hourglass-shaped and cylindrical drum (ERDWEG p. 303 fig. 202)	Tumleo
VII	23.	two-legged drum (Mus. Bat. Soc. nr. 18033a)	Lake Sentani
	24.	hourglass-shaped drum ending in a fish's mouth (HADDON III p. 280 fig.)	Murray-island (Torres Straits)

Number of the plate	Number of the instrument	Name of the instrument	Origin of the instrument
	25.	hourglass-shaped drum (ERDWEG p. 303 fig. 203)	Tumleo
	26.	id. (Mus. Bat. Soc. nr. 13575)	Okaba (South-N. G.)
VIII	27.	id. (Mus. Bat. Soc. nr. 18135)	Humboldt Bay
		C. Chordophones.	
	28.	zither, made of the nerve of a sagopalm-leaf (,,Stammseitiger Musikbogen'') (NEUHAUS vol. I p. 386 fig. 308)	Kais. Augusta-river
	29.	two-stringed musical bow (MEYER and PARKINSON vol. II pl. 23 fig. 2)	Gazelle-peninsula
	30.	monochord (BUSCHAN II vol. II p. 93 pl. 60 fig. 6)	Neu-Lauenburg
		D. Aerophones.	
IX	31.	wooden trumpet with blowing-hole at one extremity (Mus. Bat. Soc. nr. 15712)	Arso
	32.	id. (Mus. Bat. Soc. nr. 18281)	Lake Sentani
	33.	id. with lateral blowing-hole (Mus. Bat. Soc. nr. 18062)	Tobadi
	34.	bamboo trumpet with blowing-hole at one extremity (Mus. Bat. Soc. nr. 16362)	Sabèri

Number of the plate	Number of the instrument	Name of the instrument	Origin of the instrument
	35.	conch-trumpet (Tritonium variegatum) with the blowing-hole at the apex (Mus. Bat. Soc. nr. 16432a)	Waropèn-coast
	36.	conch-trumpet (Strombus maximus) with a lateral blowing-hole (Mus. Bat. Soc. nr. 16432)	ibid.
X	37.	ocarina, made of a small cocoa-nut (Mus. Bat. Soc. nr. 13661)	South-coast
	38.	flute, closed at the top, open at the bottom, lateral blowing-hole (Mus. Bat. Soc. nr. 3244a)	Humboldt Bay
	39.	id. (Mus. Bat. Soc. nr. 3244b)	ibid.
	40.	id. (Mus. Bat. Soc. nr. 15568a)	Beko
	41.	id. (Mus. Bat. Soc. nr. 15568c)	ibid.
	42.	id. (Mus. Bat. Soc. nr. 15716)	Arso
XI	43.	id. (Mus. Bat. Soc. nr. 15936a)	Waabe
	44.	id. (Mus. Bat. Soc. nr. 15936b)	ibid.
	45.	id. (Mus. Bat. Soc. nr. 18023a)	Tobadi
	46.	id. (Mus. Bat. Soc. nr. 18061a)	Kaptiau
	47.	flute, open on either side, with lateral blowing-hole in the middle (DE CLERCQ and SCHMELTZ pl. XXXIX fig. 10)	North-coast

Instruments 40–46 (Beko, ibid., Arso, Waabe, ibid., Tobadi, Kaptiau) are bracketed together as North-coast.

Number of the plate	Number of the instrument	Name of the instrument	Origin of the instrument
XII	48.	flute, open at the top, closed at the bottom, no finger-holes, blown at the top (Mus. Bat. Soc. nr. 12906)	Nacheibe
	49.	id. (Mus. Bat. Soc. nr. 16066)	Oedjang North-coast
	50.	id. (Mus. Bat. Soc. nr. 16132)	Mandé
	51.	nose-flute (LUSCHAN I pl. XXXIII fig. 2)	New-Britain
	52.	id. (LUSCHAN I pl. XXXIII fig. 6)	ibid
	53.	piston-flute (SCHMIDT-ERNSTHAUSEN p. 273 fig. 2)	Finschhafen
	54.	pan-pipe (single row) (VON HORNBOSTEL I fig. fronting p. 352)	New-Ireland
	55.	id. (NEUHAUS vol. I p. 384 fig. 306a)	Kais. Augusta-river
XIII	56.	id. (NEUHAUS vol. I p. 384 fig. 306b)	ibid
	57.	id. (WIRZ III vol. I pl. XXV fig. 1)	Merauke
	58.	pan-pipe (double row) (BUSCHAN I vol. I p. 90 fig. 118)	Buka (Solomon Islands)
	59.	bundle-flute (VON HORNBOSTEL II pl. XIII)	Bougainville (Solomon Islands)
	60.	shawm, made of a folded grass-blade (,,Blättel-Instrument'') (STEPHAN and GRAEBNER p. 124)	New-Ireland
	61.	bullroarer (,,Schwirrholz'') (Mus. Bat. Soc. nr. 18615a)	
	62.	whip-instrument (cracking whip) (HADDON III p. 274 fig. 234)	Mer (Torres Straits)

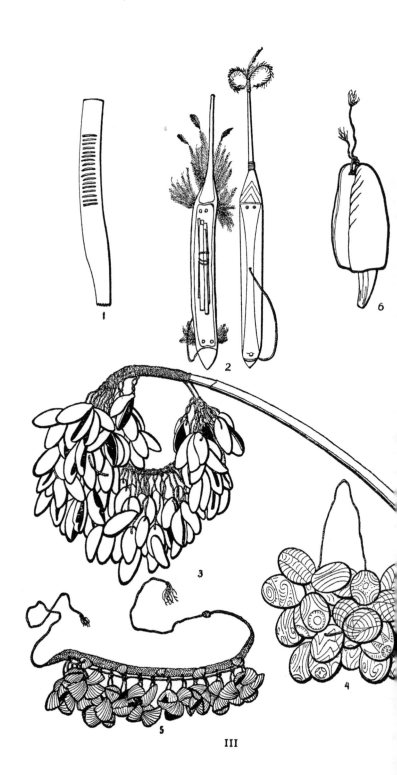

III

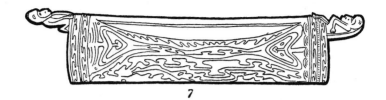

7

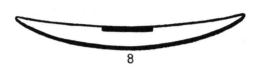

8

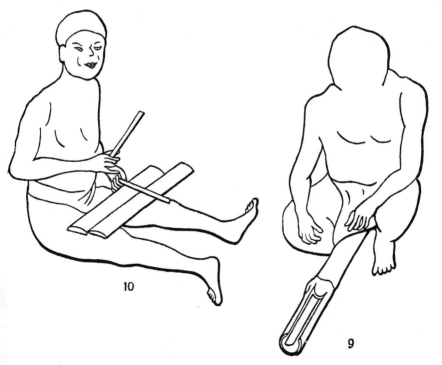

10

9

IV

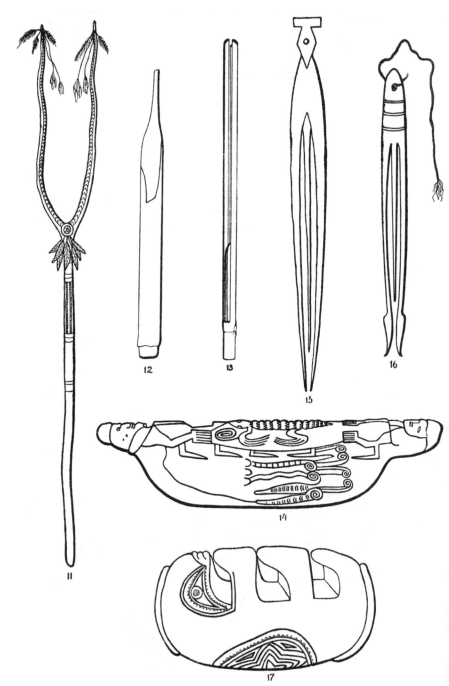

11

12

13

15

14

16

17

V

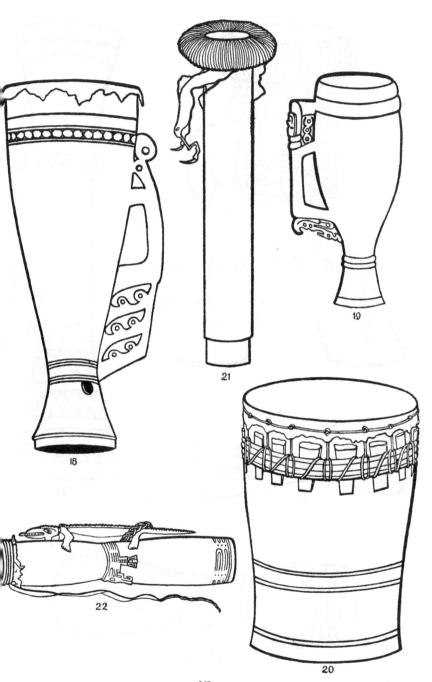

18

19

21

22

20

VI

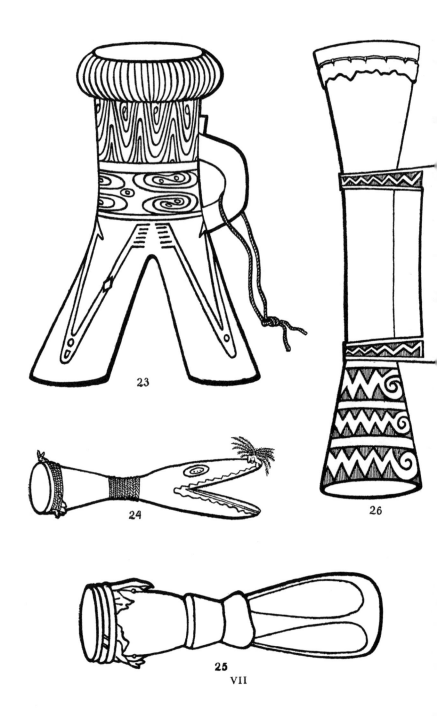

23

24

26

25

VII

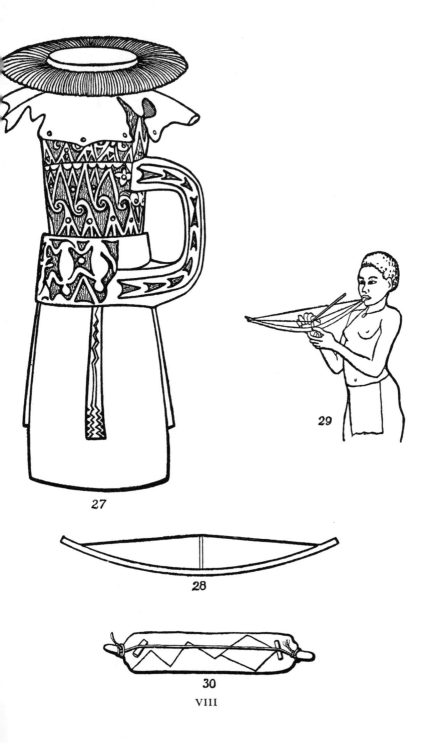

27

28

29

30

VIII

31   32   33   34

35   36

IX

38　39　40　41　42

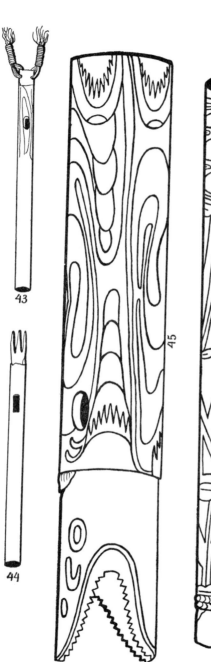

43

44

45

46

XI

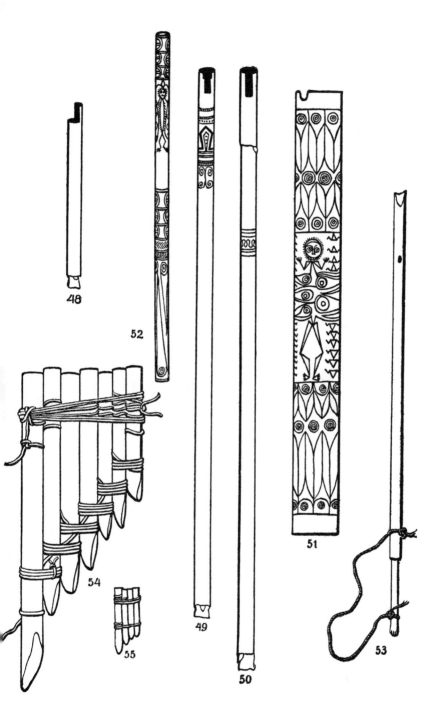

48

52

49

50

51

54

55

53

XII

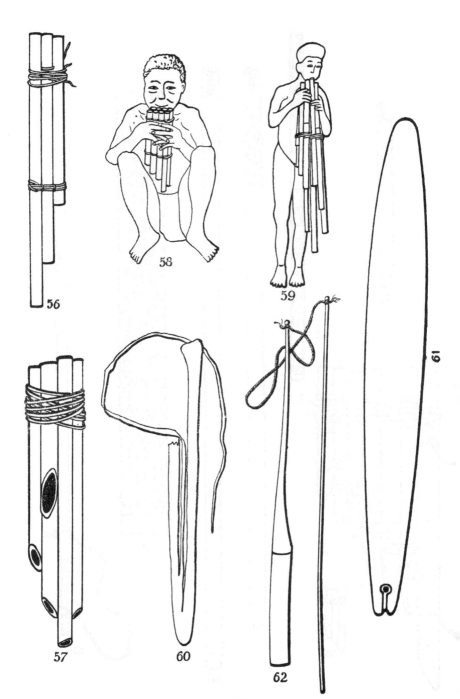

56   58   59   61

57   60   62

XIII

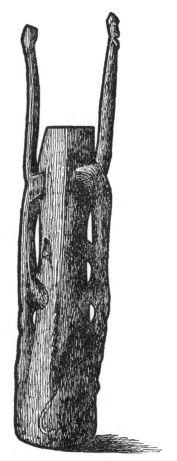

11a

XIV

BIBLIOGRAPHY
(and list of abbreviations)

Abel I   P. ABEL M. S. C., Knabenspiele auf Neu-Meck-lenburg (Südsee) ("Anthro-pos" I p. 818 a.f.), 1906.

Abel II   P. ABEL M. S. C., Knabenspiele auf Neu-Meck-lenburg (Südsee) ("Anthro-pos" II ps. 219 — 229 and 708 — 714), 1907.

d'Albertis   L. M. d'ALBERTIS, New Guinea (1880).

"Anthropos"   Internationale Zeitschrift für Völker- und Spra-chenkunde, herausgeg. unter Mitarbeit zahlreicher Missio-nare, von P. W. Schmidt S. V. D.

"Baessler-Archiv", Beitrage zur Völkerkunde, herausgeg. aus Mit-teln des Baessler-Instituts.

Baglioni   S. BAGLIONI,   Ein Beitrag zur Kenntnis der natürlichen Musik ("Globus" XCVIII ps. 232 a.f., 249 a.f., and 264 a.f.), 1910.

Van Balen   J. A. VAN BALEN, Iets over het doodenfeest bij de Papoea's aan de Geelvink-baai (1886).

Bamler   G. BAMLER,   Tami (in NEUHAUS, vol. III p. 487 a.f.) 1911.

Beaver I   W. N. BEAVER,   A description of the Girara District, Western Papua (G. J. XLIII p. 407 a.f.), 1914.

BEAVER II   W. N. BEAVER,   A further Note on the Use of the Wooden Trumpet in Pa-pua ("Man" XVI p. 23 a.f.), 1916.

Beaver III   W. N. BEAVER,   Unexplored New Guinea (1920).

Behrmann   Dr. W. BEHRMANN, Im Stromgebiet des Sepik (1922).

Bink   G. L. BINK,   Drie maanden aan de Hum-boldtbaai (T. B. G. XXXIX), 1897.

Boreel Jhr. Th. G. V. BOREEL, Reis naar Gebe, Wai-geoe (Fofagbaai en Moemoes), Dorei, Jappen (Ansoes en Am-bai), de voor de kust van Tabi liggende eilanden Wakde en Koemamba, Korrido, Mefoor, Andai, Dorei en Salawatti ("Bijdragen tot de Taal-, Land- en Volkenkunde van Neder-landsch-Indië",uitgeg. vanwege het Kon. Inst. v. d. T., L. en V. v. N. I. ter gelegenheid van het 6e Intern. Congres der Orientalisten te Leiden) p. 231 a.f. (1883).

Brandes E. W. BRANDES, Into Primeval Papua by Sea-plane ("The National Geogra-phic Magazine", vol. LVI ps. 253 a.f.), 1929.

Burger Dr. Fr. BURGER, Land und Leute auf den süd-östlichen Molukken, dem Bis-marckarchipel und den Salo-mo-Inseln ("Koloniale Ab-handlungen", Heft 72/74), (without date).

Buschan I Dr. G. BUSCHAN, Die Sitten der Völker, vol. I (1914).

Buschan II Dr. G. BUSCHAN, Illustrierte Völkerkunde, vol. II (1923).

C. A. E. Reports of the Cambridge Anthropological Ex-pedition to Torres Straits, vol. IV, Arts and Crafts (1912).

Chalmers J. CHALMERS, Notes on the natives of Kiwai Island, Fly-River, British New Guinea ("Journal of the Anthropological Institute" XXXIII), 1903.

Chignell A. K. CHIGNELL, An outpost in Papua (1911).

Chinnery E. W. P. CHINNERY, Further notes on the Use of the Wooden Kipi Trumpet and Conch Shell by the natives of Papua ("Man" XVII, p. 73 nr. 55), 1917.

De Clercq and Schmeltz, F. S. A. DE CLERCQ, with the collaboration of J.D.E. SCHMELTZ, Ethno-graphische beschrijving van de West- en Noordkust van Neder-landsch Nieuw-Guinea (1893).

Coenen J. A. W. COENEN, Rapport betreffende Britsch-Nieuw-Guinea (Papua) ("Me-ded. Encycl. Bureau" vol. XVI), 1918.

83

Detzner

H. DETZNER, Vier Jahre unter Kannibalen (1921).

Van Dissel I,

J. S. A. VAN DISSEL, Landreis van Fakfak naar Sekar (West Nieuw-Guinea) ("Indische Gids" XXVI vol. I p. 932 a.f.), 1904.

Van Dissel II

J. S. A. VAN DISSEL, Reis van Goras langs de Bedide naar Ginaroe en over Wonéra naar Goras terug. (T. A. G. XXIV p. 992 a.f.), 1907.

Eberlein

P. J. EBERLEIN M. S. C., Die Trommelsprache auf der Gazelle-Halbinsel (Neu-Pommern) ("Anthropos" V p. 635), 1910.

Van Eerde

J. C. VAN EERDE, Ethnographische gegevens van de exploratie-detachementen op Nieuw-Guinea (T.A.G. XXVIII p. 929 a.f.), 1911.

Eingeborenen Queenslands, Die ("Globus" LVI p. 119 a.f.) 1899.

Encycl. of N. I.

Encyclopaedie van Nederlandsch-Indië, vol. II 2d ed. p. 812 a.f. (834b—835b) s.v. Muziek en Muziekinstrumenten (bij Joh. F. Snelleman), (1918).

id.

vol. III 2d ed. p. 298 a.f., s.v. Papoea's (by ?), 1919.

Erdweg

M. J. ERDWEG, Die Bewohner der Insel Tumleo, Berlinhafen, Deutsch Neu-Guinea ("Mitteilungen der Anthropologischen Gesellschaft in Wien", XXXII, p. 274 a.f.), 1902.

Ethnografische gegevens betreffende de inboorlingen in het stroomgebied van de Mamberamo (Nieuw-Guinea) (T. A. G. XXXII, p. 655 a.f.), 1915.

Exploration-report,

Verslag van de militaire exploratie van Nederlandsch Nieuw-Guinea, 1907 — 1915 (1920).

Fahrt der holländischen Grenzexpedition auf den Kaiserin Augusta-Fluss, Die, ("Globus" XCVIII ps. 376 a.f.), 1910.

Feuilletau de Bruyn W. K. H. FEUILLETAU DE BRUYN, Schouten- en Padaido-eilanden ("Mededeelingen van het Encyclopaedisch Bureau" nr. 21), 1920.

Finsch I	Dr. O. FINSCH,	Neu-Guinea und seine Bewohner (1865).
Finsch II	Dr. O. FINSCH,	Ethnologischer Atlas, Typen aus der Steinzeit Neu-Guinea's (1888).
Finsch III	Dr. O. FINSCH,	Ethnologische Erfahrungen und Belegstücke aus der Südsee ("Annalen der K. K. naturhist. Hofmus. Wien", vol. III (1888), vol. VI (1891), and vol. VIII (1893).
Finsch IV	Dr. O. FINSCH,	Südseearbeiten (Abhandl. Hamb. Kol. Inst. vol. XIV), 1914.
Fischer I	H. W. FISCHER,	Een rammelaar als hulpmiddel bij de vischvangst (I. A. E. XVIII p. 179), 1908.
Fischer II	H. W. FISCHER,	Beiträge zur Ethnographie von Neu-Guinea (I. A. E. XXII), 1915.
Fischer III	H. W. FISCHER,	Ethnographica aus Süd- und Südwest-Neu-Guinea (N. G. VII p. 37), 1923.
Frazer	J. G. FRAZER,	The belief in immortality (1913).
Friederici I	G. FRIEDERICI,	Wissenschaftliche Ergebnisse einer amtlichen Forschungsreise nach dem Bismarckarchipel im Jahre 1908 (Mitteilungen aus den Deutschen Schutzgebieten, Erg. Heft 5), 1912.
Friederici II	G. FRIEDERICI,	Mitteilungen aus den Deutschen Schutzgebieten, (Erg. Heft 7), 1913.
Frizzi	E. FRIZZI,	Ein Beitrag zur Ethnologie von Bougainville und Buka mit spezieller Berücksichtigung der Nasioi ("Baessler Archiv", Beiheft VI p. 49 a.f. and "Anhang"), 1914.
Fuhrmann	E. FUHRMANN,	Neu-Guinea (Folkwangverlag, Kulturen der Erde Bd. XIV), 1922.
G. J.		Geographical Journal.
Gjellerup I	K. GJELLERUP,	De Saweh-stam der Papoea's in Noord-Nieuw-Guinea (T. A.G. XXIX p. 171 a.f.), 1912.

Gjellerup II	K. GJELLERUP, De legende van de vernietiging door tooverij van de oorspronkelijke bevolking van het schiereiland Sarmi op de Noordkust van Nieuw-Guinea en van de herbevolking van dit schiereiland (T. B. G. LVII p. 31 a.f.), 1916.
Van der Goes	H. D. VAN DER GOES, Nieuw-Guinea, ethnographisch en natuurkundig onderzocht en beschreven (in 1858), 1862.
Gooszen	A. J. GOOSZEN, De bewoners van Nederlandsch Nieuw-Guinea ("De volken van Nederlandsch-Indië" onder redactie van Prof. J. C. van Eerde, vol. II p. 104 a.f.), 1921.
Goudswaard	A. GOUDSWAARD, De Papoewa's van de Geelvinkbaai (1863).
Graebner I	F. GRAEBNER, Holztrommeln des Ramu-Distriktes auf Neu-Guinea ("Globus" LXXXIV, p. 299 a.f.), 1902.
Graebner II	F. GRAEBNER, Kulturkreise und Kulturschichten in Ozeanien (Z. F. E. vol. XXXVII, p. 28 a.f.), 1905.
Guppy	H. B. GUPPY, The Solomon Islands and their natives (1887).
HADDON I	Prof. A. C. HADDON, The Ethnography of the Western Tribes of Torresstreet ("Journal of the Anthropological Institute of Gr. Britain and Ireland"), 1890.
Haddon II	Prof. A. C. HADDON, Studies in the anthropogeography of British New-Guinea (G. J. vol. XVI p. 265 a.f., and p. 414 a.f.), 1900.
Haddon III	Prof. A. C. HADDON, Sound-producing instruments (C. A. E. ps. 270 — 283), 1912.
Haddon IV	Prof. A. C. HADDON, Notes on Wooden trumpets in New-Guinea ("Man" XVII p. 77 a.f. nr. 56), 1917.
Hagen	B. HAGEN, Unter den Papua's (1899).

Van Hasselt   F. J. F. VAN HASSELT, In het land van de Papoea's (1926).

Van Hille   J. W. VAN HILLE, Reizen in West-Nieuw-Guinea III (T. A. G. XXIV, p. 547 a.f.), 1907.

Van Hoëvell I   G. W. W. C. Baron VAN HOËVELL, De Aroe-eilanden, geographisch, ethnographisch en commerciëel (T. B. G. XXXIII p. 57 a.f.), 1890.

Van Hoëvell II   G. W. W. C. Baron VAN HOËVELL, De Kei-eilanden (T. B. G. XXXIII p. 102 a.f.), 1890.

Van Hoëvell III   G. W. W. C. Baron VAN HOËVELL, De Tanimber- en Timor-laoet-eilanden (T. B. G. XXXIII p. 160 a.f.), 1890.

Holmes   J. H. HOLMES, In primitive New Guinea (1924).

Von Hornbostel I   Prof. Dr. E. M. VON HORNBOSTEL, Notiz über die Musik der Bewohner von Süd-Neu-Mecklenburg (in Stephan und Graebner, Neu-Mecklenburg, 1907), reprinted in the "Sammelbände für vergleichende Musikwissenschaft", vol. I, p. 351 a.f.), 1922.

Von Hornbostel II   Prof. Dr. E. M. VON HORNBOSTEL, Die Musik auf den nord-westlichen Salomo-Inseln (aus dem Phonogramm-Archiv des Psychol. Instituts der Universität Berlin); Anhang zu R. Thurnwald, Forschungen auf den Salomo-Inseln und dem Bismarck-Archipel, 1912.

Von Hornbostel IIa   Prof. Dr. E. M. VON HORNBOSTEL, Ueber einige Panpfeifen aus Nordwestbrasilien (in Koch-Grünberg, Zwei Jahre unter den Indianern, p. 378 a.f.), 1910.

Von Hornbostel IIb   Prof. Dr. E. M. VON HORNBOSTEL, Ueber ein akustisches Kriterium für Kulturzusammenhänge (Z. f. E. XLIII p. 601 a.f.), 1911.

Von Hornbostel III   Prof. Dr. E. M. VON HORNBOSTEL, Melodie und Skala ("Jahrbuch der Musikbibliothek Peters", vol. XIX ps. 11 — 23), 1913.

Von Hornbostel IV Prof. Dr. E. M. VON HORNBOSTEL, Bemerkungen über einige Lieder aus Bougainville (aus dem Phonogramm-Archiv des Psych. Inst. der Univers. Berlin) ("Baessler Archiv", Beiheft VI, Anhang), 1914.

Von Hornbostel V Prof. Dr. E. M. VON HORNBOSTEL, Die Entstehung des Jodelns ("Bericht ueber den Musikwissenschaftlichen Kongress in Basel 1924", p. 203 a.f.)

Von Hornbostel VI Prof. Dr. E. M. VON HORNBOSTEL, African Negro Music (Memorandum IV of the Intern. Inst. of African Languages and Cultures, reprinted from "Africa" Vol. I No. 1), 1928.

Von Hornbostel VII Prof. Dr. E.M. VON HORNBOSTEL, Die Maassnorm als kulturgeschichtliches Forschungsmittel ("P. W. Schmidt-Festschrift" p. 303 a.f.), 1928.

Horst   Dr. D. W. HORST, Rapport van een reis naar de Noordkust van Nieuw-Guinea (1886 or '87).

Hurley   Capt. Frank HURLEY, Pearls and Savages (1924).

I. A. E.   "International Archiv für Ethnographie".

J. J. S.   De exploratie van Nieuw-Guinea (T. A. G. XXXII p. 225 a.f.), 1915.

Joest   Wilh. JOEST,   Waffe, Signalrohr oder Tabakspfeife? (I. A. E. vol. I p. 176 a.f.), 1888.

Jongejans   J. JONGEJANS,   Eenige mededeelingen omtrent den onbekenden stam der "Oeringoep" in Centraal Nieuw-Guinea ("Indië" geïll. weekblad voor Ned. en koloniën), 1921.

Keysser   Ch. KEYSSER,   Aus dem Leben der Kai-Leute (in "Neuhaus" III), 1927.

Kirschbaum   P. Fr. KIRSCHBAUM, Ein neu-entdeckte Zwergstamm auf Neu-Guinea ("Anthropos" XXII p. 202 a.f.), 1927.

Kleiweg de Zwaan	J. P. KLEIWEG DE ZWAAN, Physical anthropology in the Indian Archipelago and adjacent regions (1923).
ten Klooster	Kpt. TEN KLOOSTER, Exploratieverslag Oct./ Dec. 1911 (Archives Dept. of War).
Koch I	J. W. R. KOCH, Bijdrage tot de anthropologie der bewoners van Z. W. Nieuw-Guinea (Z. W. N. G. ps. 359 — 400), 1908.
Koch II	J. W. R. KOCH, Ethnografisch Verslag (Z. W. N. G. ps. 541 — 634), 1908.
De Kock	M. A. DE KOCK, Eenige ethnologische en anthropologische gegevens omtrent een dwergstam in het bergland van Zuid-Nieuw-Guinea (T. A. G. XXIX p. 154 a.f.), 1912.
Koning	D. A. P. KONING, Eenige gegevens omtrent land en volk der noord-oost-kust van Nederlandsch Nieuw-Guinea, genaamd Papoea Telandjang (1903).
Kopstein	Dr. F. KOPSTEIN, Zoölogische Tropenreise (without date).
Krämer	A. KRAMER, Die Malanggane von Tombara (1925).
Krämer-Bannow	E. KRÄMER-BANNOW, Bei kunstsinnigen Kannibalen (1916).
Krieger	Dr. M. KRIEGER, Neu-Guinea (1899).
Kunst I	Dr. J. KUNST, Over Soendaneesche zang-muziek ("Feestbundel, uit-gegeven door het Kon. Bat. Gen. bij gelegenheid van zijn 150-jarig bestaan 1778—1928" p. 393 a.f.), 1929.
Kunst II	Dr. J. KUNST, De l'origine des échelles musicales javano-balinaises ("Journal of the Siam Society" vol. XXIII p. 111 a.f.), 1929.
Lachmann	Dr. R. LACHMANN, Musik der aussereuropäischen Natur- und Kultur-völker (in Bücken, Hand-buch der Musikwissenschaft, Lief. 35), 1929.

Landtmann	Gunnar LANDTMANN, The Kiwai Papuans of British New Guinea (1927).
Lehner	S. LEHNER, Bukaua (in ,,Neuhaus'' vol. III p. 395 a.f.) 1911.
Lorentz	Mr. H. A. LORENTZ, Eenige maanden onder de Papoea's (1905).
Luschan I	F. VON LUSCHAN, Beiträge zur Völkerkunde der Deutschen Schutzgebiete (1897).
Luschan II	F. VON LUSCHAN, Beiträge zur Ethnographie von Neu-Guinea (1899).
Luschan III	F. VON LUSCHAN, Zur Ethnographie des Kaiserin Augusta-flusses (''Baessler Archiv'' I, ps. 103 — 117), 1911.
Maclay	N. VON MIKLUCHO MACLAY, Ethnologische Bemerkungen über die Papuas der Maclay-Küste in Neu-Guinea (''Natuurkundig Tijdschrfit voor N. I.'', p. 294 a.f.), 1876.
''Man''	A monthly record of anthropological science, published under the direction of the Royal Anthropological Institute of Great Britain and Ireland.
Martin	K. MARTIN, Reisen in den Molukken, in Ambon, den Uliassern, Seran (Ceram) und Buru (1894).
Med. Encycl. Bur.	Mededeelingen van het N.I. Encyclopaedisch Bureau
Mersch Strong	see Seligmann.
Meyer	Meyers Lexikon 7th ed. (1928).
Meyer and Parkinson	A. B. MEYER und R. PARKINSON, Album von Papua-typen (Neu-Guinea und Bismarck-Archipel), 1st vol. 1894, 2d. vol. 1900.
Murray	Sir Hubert MURRAY, Papua of to-day (1925).
Mus. Bat. Soc.	Ethnographic Museum of the ''Kon. Bataviaasch Genootschap''.
Myers	Charles S. MYERS, Music (C. A. E. ps. 238 — 269), 1912.
Neuhaus	Prof. Dr. R. NEUHAUS, Deutsch Neu-Guinea (1911).

Newton	H. NEWTON,	In far New Guinea (1914).
N. G.	Nova Guinea,	Résultats des expéditions scientifiqres à la Nouvelle Guinée, publiés sous la direction de M. le Dr. L. F. de Beaufort et de M. M. les Dr. A. A. Pulle et L. Rutten.
Parkinson I	R. PARKINSON,	Im Bismarck-Archipel. Erlebnisse und Beobachtungen auf der Insel Neu-Pommern (1887).
Parkinson II	R. PARKINSON,	Die Berlinhafen-Section, Kaiser Wilhelmsland (I. A. E. vol. XIII), 1900.
Parkinson III	R. PARKINSON,	Dreissig Jahre in der Südsee (1926).
Peekel I	P. G. PEEKEL,	Religion und Zauberei auf dem mittleren Neu-Mecklenburg (1910).
Peekel II	P. G. PEEKEL,	Das Zweigeschlechterwesen ("Anthropos" XXIV p. 1005 a.f.), 1929.
Pöch I	Dr. R. PÖCH	Beobachtungen ueber Sprache, Gesänge und Tänze der Monumbo anlässlich phonographischer Aufnahmen in Deutsch-Neu-Guinea (Mitteill. der Anthropol. Gesellsch. in Wien XXXV p. 230 a.f.), 1905.
Pöch II	Dr. R. PÖCH,	Reisen in Neu-Guinea in den Jahren 1904 — 1906 (Z.f.E. XXXIX p. 382 a.f.), 1907.
Pöch III	Dr. R. PÖCH,	Travels in German, British and Dutch New-Guinea (G. J. XXX p. 609 a.f.), 1907.
Pöch IV	Dr. R. PÖCH,	Wanderungen im nördlichen Teile von Süd-Neu-Mecklenburg ("Globus" XCIII p. 7 a.f.), 1908.
Pöch V	Dr. R. PÖCH,	Reisen an der Nordküste von Kaiser Wilhelmsland ("Globus" XCIII p. 139 a.f., 149 a.f., 169 a.f.) 1908.
Pratt	A. E. PRATT,	Two years among New Guinea cannibals (1906).

Pulle	Prof. Dr. A. PULLE, Naar het Sneeuwgebergte van Nieuw-Guinea met de derde Nederlandsche expeditie (without date; probably ed. in 1914).
Rawling I	C. G. RAWLING, Explorations in Dutch New Guinea (G. J. XXXVIII p. 233 a.f.), 1911.
Rawling II	C. G. RAWLING, The land of the New Guinea Pygmies (1913).
Reche	Otto RECHE, Der Kaiserin Augusta-Fluss ("Ergebnisse der Südsee-Expedition 1908—'10", herausgeg. von Prof. Dr. G. Thilenius, II Ethnographie, A. Melanesien, vol. I p. 425 a.f.), 1913.
Reiber	P. J. REIBER, Kinderspiele in Deutsch Neu-Guinea ("Baessler Archiv" I, ps. 227 —256), 1911.
Reinhardt	Dr. L. REINHARDT, Kulturgeschichte des Menschen. Die Erde und die Kultur II (1913).
Ribbe	C. RIBBE, Zwei Jahre unter den Kannibalen der Salomo-Inseln (1903).
Roesicke I	Dr. A. ROESICKE'S foto's from the Kais. Augustariver tribes (in the possession of Prof. Von Hornbostel).
Roesicke II	Dr. A. ROESICKE, Mitteilungen über ethnonographische Ergebnisse der Kaiserin Augusta-Fluss-Expedition (Z.f.E. XLVI p. 507 a.f.), 1914.
Van der Roest	J. L. D. VAN DER ROEST, Uit het leven der bevolking van Windèsi (Ned. Nw.-Guinea) (T. B. G. XL), 1897.
Le Roux	Ch. LE ROUX, Expeditie naar het Nassaugebergte in Centraal Noord-Nieuw-Guinea (T. B. G. LXVI, ps. 447 — 513), 1926.
Sachs I	Prof. Dr. Curt SACHS, Reallexikon der Musikinstrumente, zugleich ein Polyglossar für das gesammte Instrumentengebiet (1913).

Sachs II   Prof. Dr. Curt SACHS. Die Musikinstrumente In-
diens und Indonesiens, 1st
ed. (1915).

Sachs III   Prof. Dr. Curt SACHS, Geist und Werden der
Musikinstrumente (1929).

Sachse   F. J. P. SACHSE, Seran (Meded. Encyclopaedisch Bureau No. 29), 1922.

Van der Sande   G. A. J. VAN DER SANDE, Uitkomsten der Ne-
derlandsche Nieuw-Guinea-
expeditie in 1903 onder leiding
van Prof. A. WICHMANN,
vol. III, Ethnography and
Anthropology (N. G. III),
1907.

Sanduhrförmigen Trommeln der Matty-Insel, Die, ("Globus" XCII p.
20 a.f.), 1907.

Saville   W. J. V. SAVILLE, In unknown New Guinea,
with an introduction by Bro-
nislaw Malinowski (1926).

Schellong I   Dr. O. SCHELLONG, Musik und Tanz der Papua's ("Globus" LVI, p. 81).
1889.

Schellong II   Dr. O. SCHELLONG, Das Barlumfest der Gegend
Finschhafens (I. A. E. II blz.
145), 1889.

Schlaginhaufen   Dr. O. SCHLAGINHAUFEN, Eine ethnographische Sammlung vom Kaiserin
Augusta-Fluss in Neu-Guinea
(1910).

Schmeltz I   Dr. J. D. E. SCHMELTZ, Beiträge zur Ethnographie von Neu-Guinea (I.
A. E. VIII), 1895.

Schmeltz II   Dr. J. D. E. SCHMELTZ, Das Schwirrholz (1896).

Schmeltz III   Dr. J. D. E. SCHMELTZ, Die Stämme an der
Südküste von Niederl. Neu-
Guinea (I. A. E. XVI; p. 193
a.f.), 1904.

Schmeltz IV   Dr. J. D. E. SCHMELTZ, Beiträge zur Ethnographie von Neu-Guinea (I. A.
E. XVI, p. 224 a.f.), 1904.

Schmeltz V   Dr. J. D. E. SCHMELTZ, Ueber einige Gegen-
stände von Nord-Neu-Guinea
(I. A. E. XVI, p. 242 a.f.),
1904.

Schmeltz VI   Dr. J. D. E. SCHMELTZ, Beiträge zur Ethnographie von Neu-Guinea (I. A. E.
XVII, p. 194 a.f.), 1905.

Schmidt I   P. W. SCHMIDT, S. V. D., Die geheime Jünglingsweihe der Karesau-Insulaner (Deutsch Neu-Guinea) ("Anthropos" II, ps. 1029 — 1056), 1907.

Schmidt II   P. W. SCHMIDT, S. V. D. Ueber Musik und Gesänge der Karesau-Papua's, Deutsch Neu-Guinea (Handl. Kongress der Intern. Musikgesellschaft, Wien 1910), p. 297 a.f.

Schmidt III   P. W. SCHMIDT, S. V. D. Beiträge zur Ethnographie des Gebietes von Potsdamhafen ("Globus" LXXXIV p. 76 a.f.), 1903.

Joseph Schmidt I P. J. SCHMIDT, S. V. D., Die Ethnographie der Nor-Papua (Murik-Kaup-Karau) bei Dallmannhafen, Neu-Guinea ("Anthropos" XVIII — XIX, ps. 700 a.f.), 1923/4.

Joseph Schmidt II P. J. SCHMIDT, S. V. D., Die Ethnographie der Nor-Papua (Murik-Kaup-Karau) bei Dallmannhafen, Neu-Guinea ("Anthropos" XXI p. 49 a.f.), 1926.

Schmidt-Ernsthausen V. SCHMIDT-ERNSTHAUSEN, Ueber die Musik der Eingebornen von Deutsch Neu-Guinea ("Vierteljahrschrift für Musikwissenschaft" VI, p. 268 a.f.), 1890.

Schultze Jena Dr. L. SCHULTZE JENA, Forschungen im innern der Insel Neu-Guinea (1914).

Seligmann I   C. G. SELIGMANN, A classification of the Natives of British New Guinea ("Journal of the Royal Anthrop. Inst. of Gr. Britain and Ireland" XXXIX p. 314 a.f.), 1909.

Seligmann II C. G. SELIGMANN, The Melanesians of British New-Guinea (1910).

Seligmann III C. G. SELIGMANN, Note on a wooden Horn or Trumpet from British New-Guinea ("Man" XV p. 22 a.f.), 1915.

Seligmann and Mersh Strong, C. G. SELIGMANN, and W. MERSH STRONG, Anthropogeographical investigations in British New-Guinea (G. J. XXVII, p. 225 a.f.), 1906.

Snelleman   Joh. F. SNELLEMAN, Muziek en Muziekinstrumenten (Encycl. v. N. I.
vol. II 2nd ed. p. 812 (834b —
835b)), 1918.

Stanley   E. R. STANLEY, New Guinea (in Brouwer,
Practical Hints to Scientific
Travellers, vol. III, p. 121
a.f.), 1925.

Stephan   E. STEPHAN,   Südseekunst (1907).

Stephan and Graebner Dr. E. STEPHAN und Dr. R. GRAEBNER,
Neu-Mecklenburg (1907).

Stroeve   Lt. t. Zee J. Th. STROEVE, Exploratieverslag 7
Febr. — 13 Mrt. 1914 (Ar-
chives Dept. of War).

T. A. G.   "Tijdschrift van het Kon. Nederlandsch Aard-
rijkskundig Genootschap".

Tauern   O. D. TAUERN, Patasiwa und Patalima
(1918).

T. B. G.   "Tijdschrift voor Indische Taal-, Land- en Vol-
kenkunde", ed. by the "Kon.
Bataviaasch Genootschap van
Kunsten en Wetenschappen."

Thilenius I   Prof. Dr. G. THILENIUS, Ethnographische Pseu-
domorphosen in der Südsee
("Globus" LXXXI p. 117
a.f.), 1902.

Thilenius II   Prof. Dr. G. THILENIUS, Alfred C. Haddon'
Forschungen auf den Inseln
der Torresstrasse und in Neu-
Guinea ("Globus" LXXXI
p. 327 a.f.), 1902.

Thomson   J. P. THOMSON, British New-Guinea (1892).

Thurnwald I   Dr. R. THURNWALD, Der Gemeinde der Bana-
ro; Ehe, Verwandtschaft und
Gesellschaftsbau eines Stam-
mes im Innern von Neu-
Guinea (Aus der Ergebnissen
einer Forschungsreise 1913 —
'15), 1921.

Thurnwald II   Dr. R. THURNWALD, Im Bismarckarchipel
und auf den Salomo-inseln
1906 — 1909 (Z. f. E. XLII
p. 98 a.f.), 1910.

Thurnwald III   Dr. R. THURNWALD, Forschungen auf den Salomo-Inseln und dem Bis-
marck-Archipel (1912).

Tillema   H. F. TILLEMA, Kromoblanda, vol. IV (1921).

Tissot   J. W. TISSOT VAN PATOT, Een viertal tochten door het eiland Terangan (Aroe-eilanden) in Maart en April 1907 (T. A. G., 2nd series XXV p. 77 a.f.), 1908.

Valentijn   François VALENTIJN's "Oud en Nieuw Oost-Indiën" reprinted by Mr. S. Keyzer, 2nd ed. 1862.

Vertenten   P. VERTENTEN, Zeichen und Malkunst der Marindinesen. (I. A. E. XXII p. 149 a.f.), 1915.

Vormann I   P. Fr. VORMANN, S. V. D. Tänze und Tanzfestlichkeiten der Monumbo-Papua (Deutsch Neu-Guinea) ("Anthropos" VI, p. 411 a.f.), 1911.

Vormann II   P. Fr. VORMANN, S. V. D. Das tägliche Leben der Papua (unter besonderer Berücksichtigung des Valman-Stammes auf Deutsch Neu-Guinea) ("Anthropos" XII — XIII p. 891 a.f.), 1917/8.

Wasterval   J. A. WASTERVAL, Een en ander omtrent godsdienst, zeden en gewoonten bij de bevolking in en omtrent de Humboldtbaai (T. B. G. LXI p. 499 a.f.), 1922.

Werner   Dr. E. WERNER, Kaiser-Wilhelms-Land (1911)

Williams I   F. E. WILLIAMS, The Vailala Madness and the destruction of native ceremonies in the Gulf Division ("Anthropology", Report Nr. 4 of the Territory of Papua), 1923.

Williams II   F. E. WILLIAMS, The natives of the Purari Delta ("Anthropology" Report Nr. 5 of the Territory of Papua), 1924.

Williams III   F. E. WILLIAMS, Orokaiva-magic (1928).

Williamson,   Robert W. WILLIAMSON, The Mafulu, Mountain people of British New-Guinea, with an introduction by A. C. Haddon (1912).

Winthuis   J. WINTHUIS, Das Zweigeschlechterwezen (1927).

Wirz I   Dr. P. WIRZ, Dies und jenes über die Sentanier und die Geheimkulte im Norden von Neu-Guinea (T. B. G. LXIII p. 1 a.f.), 1923.

Wirz II	Dr. P. WIRZ,	Anthropologische und ethnologische Ergebnisse der Central-Neu-Guinea Expedition 1921 — '22 (N. G. p. 1 a. f. XVI), 1924.
Wirz III	Dr. P. WIRZ,	Die Marinde-anim von Holländ. Süd-Neu-Guinea (1922/'25).
Wirz IV	Dr. P. WIRZ,	Dämonen und Wilde in Neu-Guinea (1928).
Wirz V	Dr. P. WIRZ,	Beitrag zur Ethnologie der Sentanier, Holländisch Neu-Guinea (N. G. XVI p. 251 a.f.), 1928.
Wirz VI	Dr. P. WIRZ,	Bei liebenswürdigen Wilden in Neu-Guinea (1929).
Wollaston I	A. F. R. WOLLASTON, Pygmies and Papuans (1912).	
Wollaston II	A. F. R. WOLLASTON, An Expedition to Dutch New-Guinea (G. J. XLIII p. 248 a. f.), 1914.	
Z. f. E.	Zeitschrift für Ethnologie, Organ der Berliner Gesellschaft für Anthropologie und Urgeschichte.	
Z. W. N. G.	The South-West New-Guinea-Expedition of the ''Kon. Nederlandsch Aardrijkskundig Genootschap'' (1908).	

CORRIGENDA.

p. 43, note 74, 4th line, to be read: *East,* instead of *Eeat;*

p. 45, note 79, to be read: Together with its very remarkable series of tones, derived from an old Chinese scalar system, it has found its way... etc.;

note 80, 2nd line, to be read *sixth,* instead of *third;*

p. 71, 2nd column, the symbol ⊓ to be read: ⊟.